Searching for Odo by

Mary Mensah

All Scripture quotations, unless otherwise indicated, are taken from the Authorized (King James) Version.

Book design by Sjayartistry

ISBN (paperback) 979-8-9904062-5-4
ISBN (eBook) 979-8-9904062-4-7

Glossary

Word/Phrases	Meaning
Odo	Love
Akoma	Heart (Adinkra symbol for love.)
me nhu wo akyɛ	I haven't seen you in a long time.
ɛdeɛn na ɛrekɔ so?	What's going on?
Kafra/Kose	Sorry
Do my mates have two heads?	an expression used for when people are doing better than you.
yɛwɔ abɔnten	We are outside. Often used to signify that people are out, partying, or enjoying themselves.
Ɛyɛ asɛm oo	it's an issue/problem.
fa kyɛ wo yɔnko	Forgive your neighbor.
wo ho te sɛn?	How are you?
adɛn?	Why?
Ɛyɛ ya	It is painful
Fa ma Nyame, nsu	Leave it to God, don't cry
ɔdɔ behu wo	Love will find you.
fa wo koma to wo yam	Take heart
Wotee deɛ mekae no?	Did you hear what I said?
Kokonsa	gossiper
Ei! Ei!	Used to express intense emotion and surprise/shock.
Wonders shall never end	Express shock and astonishment.
Awurade Nyame	God
Nante Yie	Safe Journey
Ete sen	What's up
me ho yɛ	I'm well.
medaase	Thank you.
gye gye w'ani	Live and enjoy life.
Ginger you up	to excite, motivate, energize, or boost someone's morale
Abronoma	Dove
Trotro	a privately owned minibus used for shared, low-cost public transportation in Ghana and parts of West Africa
mesoo daeɛ bi faa wo ho	I had a dream about you.
Na wo ne aberante bi wɔ hɔ	You were with a young man.
Wa ma makoma nto me yam	You have given me peace of mind.
Sa abranteɛ wei yɛ serious	This guy is serious.
Gele/Duku	Traditional, often stiff, fabric head wraps
Make my head swell	Making someone become overly proud due to excessive praise.
Yen gye nnooma?	Should we accept these items?
Aane mo'n gye nnooma. sɛ woannye nneɛma yi a obiara endidi nnɛ	Yes, accept the items. If you do not, nobody will eat today.
Ayeeko	Well done/congratulations.
Ahoɔfɛ	Beautiful

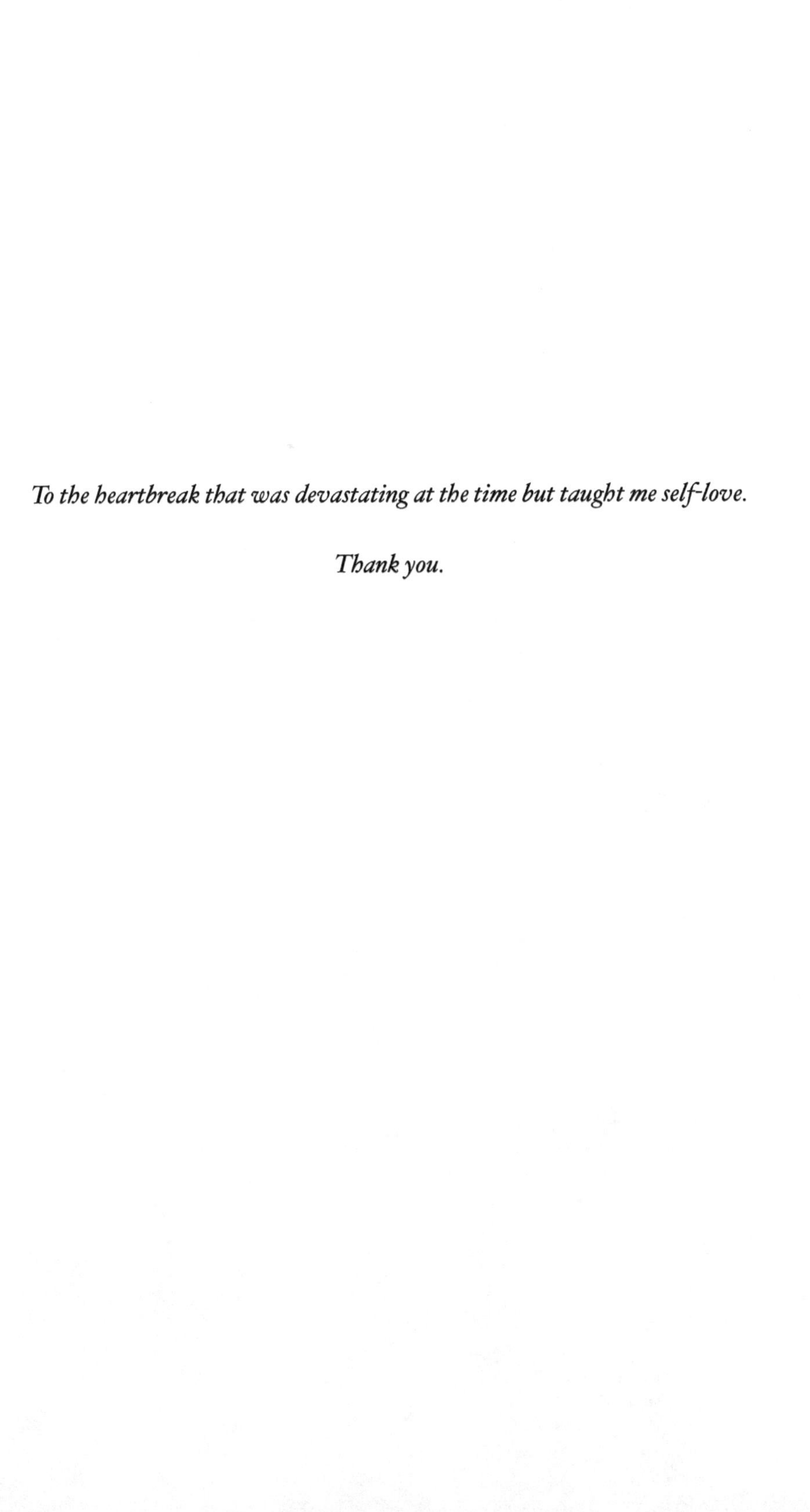

To the heartbreak that was devastating at the time but taught me self-love.

Thank you.

Chapter One

YOU JUST LOST A GOOD ONE

"Choose me! Adore me! You just see through me. You never truly loved me, did you? Why don't you want to fight for us?" These are the words I want to say, but instead, I let out a heavy sigh. You know, I tried. I really did, but here I am, 29 going on 30, and I'm begging a man to love me the way I always wanted. How pathetic is that? Here we are in his apartment, surrounded by memories we've shared. I am in his living room remembering the time we danced to music while I was wearing his favorite basketball jersey. I want to cling to those moments. The room feels so bare. I look around at his wall and see the two framed pictures of us are taken down. The one above his nice leather couch and the other next to it. My heart hurts in this moment because of what's about to happen next. The song "Official Girl" by Cassie plays in my head. The nature of the lyrics makes me realize I was never his priority. Oh, how I wanted to be his number one pick, but instead, I am stuck with the belief that I am never chosen. "Seth, you know you really broke me." I cry, unable to control myself.

"So what? I'm not the one for you, Esi. Why can't you see that?" he replies. I want to hurt him, but no matter how hard I try, I couldn't.

Seth and I have been together for about three years. He threw everything we had away. Every time I would bring up marriage, he would avoid the conversation altogether or start an argument.

He would always say, "Esi, all you think about is marriage. What if I told you, it wouldn't be for a while? Why are you stressing me?" He would scowl each time.

Tear drops roll down my cheek, and as I wipe them away, I know this is the last time I'll see him. All I could think about was the smell of his Burberry cologne I got him captivating the air. This was the end of everything. The love we shared meant nothing to him. It wasn't enough to make him stay, and I wasn't going to let him tell me again that he didn't want me.

"Esi, can you hear me?" Seth says.

I was so lost in thought I was hardly listening to him. *I think I'm going to be sick. I have to go home.*

"Esi, please talk to me. What's going on?"

Oh, now you care? What happened to telling me to get over our relationship? I think. I look on my phone and open the Uber app. I request the Uber right away. It's coming in five minutes. *Calm down Esi, this is just a bad dream. Things will be better in the morning.*

My head is filled with thoughts questioning the existence of everything. Was this relationship real? Why must he tell me this news shy of our anniversary? A month later, and it will be my birthday. What a way to bring in the new decade of my life. He told me just days before that I was amazing and how he loved me. That was Valentine's Day when he showered me with so much praise. Was that even true? Men always know what to say to make you fall for them. February 23rd: that's the date my life changed as I knew it.

A couple minutes later, my Uber is here. I gather my stuff and slam the door. I don't look back. I don't even bother replying to him calling me out of my name or using obscene language. I'm not going to sit around talking about a dead situation. Seth already told me he wanted to break up, I just have to accept it. As I'm in the Uber I think to myself, *why doesn't anyone love me?* The more I think about it, the more nauseous I feel during my ride. *Breathe*, I tell myself, *the ride will be over soon.*

Finally, we approach my building, and I feel better. I thank the driver and run up to my apartment, which is on the fourth floor. I could've taken the elevator, but didn't feel like waiting or interacting with anyone. As soon as I enter my apartment, all the emotions come flooding through my mind. I was no longer nauseous, but all I want to do is cry.

Tears begin falling from my eyes. During this time, all the memories of Seth flooded my mind, which made me cry even more. I mean, we had our good moments, but I guess that couldn't stop him from breaking up with me. How will I move on from this? My parents were expecting him to propose. What will I tell them?

Just when I was lost in thought, I get a call from Zuhrah, my bestie. I'm thinking, *what it could be*, so I answer the phone.

"Esi, how are you? me nhu wo akyɛ. ɛdeɛn na ɛrekɔ so?"

It's times like this I wish I didn't have to say what's wrong with me. There's a long pause before I tell her the news. In that time, I'm contemplating what to say.

"Zuhrah, you know Seth... well, he just broke up with me."

She was dumbfounded, unable to speak. She was the main one rooting for us to get married. This also broke her to see me distraught. All she said was *kafra*. "Esi Owusu-Ansah, tell me what happened? This doesn't make sense," she said. When Zuhrah calls me by my full name, you know she means business.

"I don't even know where to start. Well, Seth invited me to his house and said he needed to talk after my work shift. I suspected he was up to something, but wasn't sure. We had normal conversation, then he says, 'Esi you know I haven't been happy in this relationship for the last year.' I began to brace myself for what will happen next.

"He proceeded to say that he would like to break up, which brought tears to my eyes. After that, I told him how he broke me. He didn't seem to care, telling me I should get over it. Everything after that was a blur. I grabbed my things and left, not looking back. I knew it was over when he didn't even say, 'let's make this relationship work.'"

I feel like a fool wasting three years on a relationship only for it to not end in marriage. I say this out loud, which hurts me to my core. *I mean, do my mates have two heads? Why do others get what they want except me?* I thought.

Zuhrah tells me it's not my fault that Seth was a jerk and doesn't feel the same way about me anymore. That it's up to me to live my best life regardless of if I have a man.

It's easy for her to say; she has a man, and he just proposed to her a month ago. I was waiting for my turn, but I guess it won't happen at all. Zuhrah says my name, and I respond.

She says, "Esi, I will keep you in my prayers, but always remember that someone's inability to love you doesn't determine your self-worth." I hear her, but my mind isn't comprehending those words.

The phone call ends, and I lay in my bed, crying and wondering, *why am I so unlovable?* I know it's not true, but this feeling has come over me and I don't know how to shake it. Every relationship I've been in has left me broken and feeling unworthy of love in the end. The men I have been with have all stated I'd look better if I lost weight. If I changed the essence of my being, they'd love me more. When I said anything, they'd say, 'oh, you know I love you,' and only say it because I care. I have had such an unhealthy obsession with food and diet culture due to this. They amplified my insecurities to the extent I kept questioning the love we shared. I was never good enough for them. Building myself up and starting over is what I do each time. I don't even know how to be single and happy. Out of all of my friends and siblings, I am the single one now. What a shame.

I woke up the next morning in a daze, but I had to muster up the strength to go to work. It's around 6 am. I am a speech pathologist, which means I help students with a wide range of speech impediments. My students can't see me sad, and neither can my co-workers. I have to put on a facade like everything is okay when it's not. I wish I could stay home all day and avoid the outside world. But the show must go on regardless of my emotions.

I take a shower and put on my favorite lotion and perfume which are from Victoria Secret's Pure Seduction line. I wear my grey blazer and matching pants with a nice blouse inside. In addition to this, I wear my Coach loafers. I have to look presentable at all times, even when I don't feel my best. I make myself a quick breakfast that consists of a whole wheat bagel with Nutella and cranberry juice. I have been trying to work on my health and wellness journey for some time, which has been a task.

When I get out the door, it's 7:15 am. It usually takes me less than thirty minutes to get to the school. I happen to work for Sunrise Academy elementary school in Queens, NY. I've been working there for about two years. I love my job and what I do. I don't enjoy every moment, but my passion for the field is why I got into it. I get off the train with my handbag on my shoulder, ready to tackle the day ahead.

As soon as I enter the school building, my mood shifts. I know that I have to put up a good front for my students. I go to my office and get settled down. I'm hoping the time goes by fast. It's Friday, so you know I'm excited. I can't wait to have the weekend to do as I please. I turn on my computer and check my emails. I have some work-related stuff I have to sort out before I pick up some students. I get a knock on my door and it's Mrs. Conrad.

She is a sweet woman whose roughly five feet tall. She has a petite shape and short blonde hair. She's always concerned about others. That's the reason we get along so well. She'll check on you whenever she gets the chance. I have grown fond of her. She has become the closest person to me while working at this school. I say to come in, and she says, "Good morning, Ms. O."

At the school, they call me Ms. O because saying my full last name became too difficult. This is quite infuriating each time I try to correct them. While I do not mind teaching my coworkers my name and educating them on its pronunciation and sentimental value, it's a daunting task that no one prepares you for. Sometimes I wish they would at least try to articulate my name properly. *If they could say other people's surname with no hesitation, surely mine can't be that difficult.* Makes me realize the forces at play that make people shy away from saying ethnic names. There's a lot of things to unpack.

I respond with, "Good morning, how are you doing?"

She tells me she is doing all right, but she's ready for the day to be over. "It's been a long week," she says, and I agree.

Mrs. Conrad could sense that something is wrong with me, but instead of prying for information, she tells me this. "Ms. O, whatever is bothering you today, I hope that you can heal from it. I know it's not my place to say anything, but I care about you and want to see you happy."

I wanted to cry and tell her about my breakup, but something stopped me in my tracks.

Having work friends is great, but I learned that some things are better off unsaid. I know she means well, however, I realized a long time ago that your issues aren't meant for everyone to hear. It creates unnecessary drama and attention. Then you have people giving unwarranted advice. I'd rather be on the safe side then have my business get in the ears of the wrong people.

After she left, I went back to working on the computer. I have to pick up a student. I brought the student to my office and read with her. Mila is overcoming her difficulty with pronouncing and reading words. It's my responsibility to help her. She has made significant progress during the year I have been working with her. This school year, she has been able to apply the techniques I've taught her.

"Ms. O, you are the best teacher ever!" Mila gave me the biggest hug, which warmed my heart.

"Thank you, Mila. I'm glad." Hearing this was what I needed. It's something I love doing because it makes me feel useful. The time actually goes by fast. I have a few students today, which is convenient for me. I ate lunch, and before I knew it, school ended for the day.

I take the train back to my apartment. Once I open the door, I begin thinking of Seth again. It's like my mind reminded me of the times we spent at my apartment. As I look at the Akoma adinkra symbol above my gray sectional, I am reminded love doesn't always last. Maybe love conquers all for some, but for me, it seems like a never-ending cycle. It's difficult to see in this moment. I'm thinking about how I will break the news to my parents. Well, mainly my mom, being that she's the one asking every time we speak about marriage.

I call my mom, and she answers on the first ring. She said, "Esi wo ho te sɛn?" I knew I couldn't lie to her, so I said I wasn't feeling the best lately. She was concerned, asking, "Adɛn?"

I told her that Seth and I broke up and she said, "Oh Oh Ɛyɛ ya. Kafra."

I couldn't control my tears. I apologized to my mom because I was letting her down.

She said, "Fa ma Nyame, nsu."

I felt that deeply. At this point, casting all my burdens onto my maker is all I can do. She knew I might not want to hear this, but knowing my mom, she always believes.

My mom said, "Esi, love always follows you in the most unconventional ways. So, fa wo koma to wo yam. Wotee deɛ mekae no?"

"Yes, Mom, I heard what you said." Deep down inside, I know I might not meet another man for a while.

I will no longer feel the tender embrace of another. I thought this year was finally when I'd get proposed to. I mean, all my siblings found a spouse. Gabrielle, Ivy, and Anastasia all found someone. Why is my own so difficult? Now they will have an excuse to feel above me. There's this secret competition that my sisters have with one another. They always have to one up each other.

My sister Gabrielle was the one that told me Seth wasn't the one. She said, "Esi, I don't think Seth is part of your future. Something in my spirit is telling me this."

Did I listen to her? Well, no, because in my mind I thought she was a hater. Thinking back, I should've cut my losses with that man before he could break my heart.

Gabrielle is always right about things. It's like she has this sense about what's yet to come. Each time I would make excuses for the man and say, "That's how he is," Gabrielle would say, "Okay, if you say so, but I feel as though you're destined for much better."

My mom calls my name, and I snap out of it. She asks me what I am thinking of doing now. I really don't know. I feel hopeless, and the more I think about this breakup, the sadder I feel. I know I will be all right, but this feeling is terrible.

My mom says that I will find another guy, but in all honesty, I'm not ready to date. I don't even want to think about men for the time being. People suck! You think they care about you, until one day, that all changes. Their feelings fade and the person you knew is now a distant stranger. All of a sudden, you have to adjust to a world without them.

I put on my comfy clothes, which happen to be a pink shirt and bottoms to match with hearts all over. I tell myself that I will never let a man come between my happiness. A ring and the status of being married isn't worth it. I should have the same value in society as someone who is married. If it's meant to be, it'll happen for me. I am done with this pity party. Sure, I might be sad, but one thing about Esi: she always bounces back.

Instead of being in my feelings all day, I decide to watch TV shows on Netflix. Since I haven't sat down to watch TV in a long time. The only time I really get to relax is during the weekends. I began watching the *Good Girls* series and was hooked on it for the rest of the night. I didn't think I would like it much, being that I haven't seen it before.

The next morning, I felt good, but not my usual self. I am working towards being a better me. I will not allow this breakup to take over my life. *Easier said than done.* I mean, I have to give myself a break. Getting over a relationship isn't easy. One day I won't feel this pain. I will be in a better space mentally.

I am not broken or unworthy of love. I assumed I was just days ago, but it turns out I was wrong. I will love again, and it will be better than any situation I put myself in. I will feel loved and wanted. As I speak these words, may they come to pass in my life. No longer will I be the victim. I will be an overcomer.

I start my morning off with a prayer thanking God for where I am in my life. I also pray for divine protection for me, my friends, and family. After I'm done, I get up and take a shower. I get dressed in something breathable. Then I put on some relaxing music and light a candle, which happens to be Among the Clouds by Bath and Body Works. Immediately, the room is full of the fragrance of the candle.

I'm starting my morning off to a good start. I start thinking about what I would like to eat, but I'm not sure. I end up eating honey bunches of oats. After I'm done, I start doing a deep clean of my apartment. I put on some amazing music on my TV. I played various kinds of music starting with "No Scrubs" by TLC. I begin singing to myself as I cleaned.

It took me a few hours to get the apartment cleaned. A one-woman job ain't easy, but I make it work. I'm so tired that I couldn't bring myself to cook. So, I decide to go on my Uber Eats app and order dinner. It takes me a while to choose, but I finally settle on Popeyes. I got a classic blackened bacon and cheese chicken sandwich, fries, strawberry biscuit, and a strawberry Fanta. It was so good, but I had leftovers being that I couldn't finish the rest.

That night is spent watching TV shows and reading a book. It's a book titled *Before I Let Go*. The book is so good I can't put it down. I practically have to force myself to sleep. I wake up the next morning feeling a bit groggy. I start praying and thanking God for waking me up and protecting me through the night. I put on a sermon on my TV, which reminded me to rely on God more, for he is the author of my life.

After the sermon, I began searching up Bible quotes to encourage myself. Two stood out to me. One was Philippians 4:6, which says, "Do not be anxious about anything, but in everything by prayer and supplication with thanksgiving let your requests be known to God." The second verse happened to be 1 Peter 5:7. It reads, "cast all your anxieties on him because he cares for you."

These Bible verses uplift my spirit and give me hope. I start watching another sermon video, about dating and the red flags to watch out for. It's very interesting watching those videos, because it taught me about maintaining my self-worth. The person I'm dating should be pouring into the relationship and leading me closer to my faith.

A lot of people get into relationships with people that aren't compatible with them. I guess it's what I need to hear. Seth and I weren't well-suited for each other. We both wanted very different things. He didn't believe in marriage. He's one of those people that believe it's just a piece of paper. Despite me trying, it was a tumultuous relationship. Each time, I would be chasing the good times. You can say that we were unequally yoked.

I would constantly lie to myself, saying one day he'd change. I even thought we were soulmates. All those arguments were for nothing. He would always say he wanted to work on our relationship after. If only I knew my efforts were a waste of time, I wouldn't have progressed further. Anyways, hindsight isn't always 20/20. You can never be sure how things will pan out for you.

Especially a lover girl and hopeless romantic like me. I always ignore the red flags for the sake of love. I know I shouldn't have because this heartache is painful. Men can really suck. If you put your trust in man, it will end in disappointment. You know who will never leave nor forsake you? It's God.

I have comfort knowing he will always be there even when my world feels like it's crashing. It's times like this I think about the fact that I have been unsuccessful in love. As I go into that thought, the Tina Turner song "What's Love Got to Do With It" pops in my head. It relates to my situation so much and the lyrics mean a lot.

Sometimes I wish I could be heartless and only think about myself. I am an empath. I feel people's pain and that stops me every time I want to react negatively. When you're such a caring person, sometimes you get people that are attracted to your light. Those people drain you. You're so busy pouring into their cup, you forget about you.

A few weeks later, and I am in the rut of going to work and home. I have been doing well distracting myself. It's getting quite boring for me. I need to go out and have some fun. I got a call from Nadira, asking if I wanted to go out for brunch the next day. She is my good friend from grad school. We went to Brooklyn College together. She is short and very curvaceous, but her words pack a punch. She is into kokonsa and knows about the tea before it gets out. I trust her judgement on things, I just wish she didn't have a big mouth. It was a Friday when she asked, so I agreed. I'm wondering what I should wear.

I have an hourglass curvy shape, so I usually find things that compliment my figure. I am very particular about what I wear. I like to look elegant and timeless. I look through my closet and find this floral turquoise wrap dress. I find some white mule heels to wear and some gold accessories. I can't wait to go out with my girl.

Nadira texted me and said we will meet at 12:00 pm at the restaurant called Clinton St. Baking Co. The next morning was great. I knew

I would have an awesome time with her. I take a shower, get dressed, and put on my Sol de Janeiro Brazilian Crush Cheirosa 68 Beija Flor perfume mist. It smells so good on me. I feel classy with this outfit I put together.

I leave my apartment at around 11:30 am and decide to take an Uber there. I know I won't get there on time just taking the train because the weekend is terrible. I'm the first one to arrive to the restaurant. A few minutes later, I see my friend. She's wearing a long sleeve v-neck orange dress. Nadira is wearing her hair in an afro with a nice accessory to adorn her crown. She has beautiful mahogany skin.

She sees me and is all smiles. Nadira says, "Hey sis, OMG, I missed you."

We hug one another. After that, we get seated at a table. We look at the menu and choose our food. I get pancakes with maple butter, omelet, and a cold apple cider. While Nadira gets fried chicken and waffles, hash browns, and lemonade. While we wait for our food, we talk.

"So, Esi, tell me what has been going on with you?"

I look at her, confused. I begin biting my lip and saying, "Um, where do I start." I tell her how I have been getting over my breakup with Seth.

Nadira says, "What, you and Seth broke up? I knew my eyes weren't playing tricks on me."

I ask her what she meant by that.

Nadira pauses for a moment and says, "What I'm about to tell you will disappoint you. Please understand it wasn't intentional on my end to omit this information." Around two weeks ago, she saw Seth with another woman. They were holding hands and kissing. They didn't even notice her. She was going to tell me, but didn't know how.

I feel crushed hearing this. Not because I expected Seth and I to get back together, but that my suspicions were confirmed. *This man really played me for a fool.* A couple months ago, he started hanging out with a friend that he was reluctant to tell me about. Even when I would ask about this friend, he would never tell me. That was the first time I thought he might be cheating.

I recall one instance I tried to use his phone to take a picture. The way he spazzed out on me and snatched the phone was all the confirmation I needed to know something was up with him. I questioned him about it, and he said I shouldn't use his phone to take pictures. That I needed to use my own. I was suspicious, but I didn't make a fuss about it after that.

"He was cheating on me for months then," I tell Nadira.

She says, "I am so sorry, sis. He didn't deserve you and the fact that he treated you this way is messed up. I hope you find happiness and love so special it inspires others. I want you to believe in love again even if you can't right now."

I appreciate those words from her. Although I'm not looking for love right now, I have hope that I'll love again. This time, I will set my standards high and show myself respect.

It hurts me that he moved on so fast like what we shared meant nothing to him. I come to the realization that I can't let that get me down. I have to move on from this situation. I should start dating when I am ready. I need to heal first. I believe I am on my way towards that. Seth no longer has a hold on me. Why must I bother myself about this situation. Why does it sting to hear this information?

"Nadira what have you been up to?" I thought if I changed the subject, it would lighten the mood a bit. She says she's been working and going to outings with her other friends. She's always been fun to hang out with. She works as a nurse for a nearby hospital in The Bronx. She decided after we got our speech language pathology degrees that pursuing nursing was her passion. This woman is an inspiration being that she overcame so much in becoming who she is today. Nadira likes what she does being in the labor and delivery sector. She has compassion for others that makes her a good fit for this role.

Nadira and I talk about a lot of things. It's great catching up with her. She gives me encouraging words and tells me to keep my head up. This has me thinking about a song by Tupac Shakur. He's uplifting women to not put up with a man that can't treat you right.

Those words encourage me to move on and find myself. I must learn Esi's likes and dislikes. The things that make me who I am. I know it won't be easy, but I'm ready to move on. Been in a relationship so long I forgot about me. After we finish eating, it's time to part ways.

The food was amazing, we told each other. This is definitely our new brunch spot. We hug and then I'm on my way back home.

Once I arrive home, I decide to go through my phone and delete all the pictures of Seth and me. I finally muster the courage to delete his number and messages off my phone. I even block him on all social media accounts. I know doing this means there is no going back. I take the things he got me around my home and throw them away. I deserve to be happy too, and keeping these memories of him is stunting my growth.

I put on some music and the first song to come on is by Miley Cyrus, called "flowers." In the song she talks about self-love. I'm singing off the top of my lungs and dancing to the beat. Music speaks to my soul. In times of sorrow, it lifts my mood. Usually, I would be out at parties or gatherings. Ever since the breakup, everything reminds me that I'm single. I keep replaying the song by Stefflon Don called "Hurtin' Me" in my mind. Especially the chorus. I don't know why I care so much about what others think and ask me. This whole situation is difficult.

It's really time that I get back to living my best life. I lost the essence of who I am. In the next few months, I will be a part of Zuhrah's wedding as her maid of honor. I'm happy for her, but deep down, it pains me that it couldn't be me as well. I have been waiting for marriage only to have it taken away. Perhaps he was never going to propose, leaving me a girlfriend for years with no true commitment.

Well, I guess God doesn't want me in a relationship let alone a marriage that's not bearing fruit. It would have ended in a divorce, which is something I'm against. He wasn't right for me, but I preferred being with him than being alone. I am loyal when it comes to dating. I'll stick to one person even if we're not compatible all, because being single is lonely.

Now that I'm single, I'm feeling so isolated from everyone and everything. It's mainly my doing because I have been so emotional these past few weeks. How I deal with things is pushing people away. This doesn't help because I lose friends each time I go through my depressive episodes. I have been grieving this relationship that was over long before it even started.

keep trying to encourage myself, saying that I can get over Seth. However, each time I try, I keep thinking about him and the good times we shared. He would make me laugh. We shared lots of good banter. Time stops when I was around him, but I know he doesn't feel the same. Moving on will be difficult, but I know it's something I must do.

Chapter Two

WHAT'S LOVE?

APPROXIMATELY THREE MONTHS HAS PASSED, AND I AM SLOWLY regaining a sense of who I am. Zuhrah invited me to go wedding dress shopping with a few family members and the bridesmaids. It will be fun seeing her try on different gowns and make her choice. We decided to meet up at the first bridal shop called Woná New York.

I probably will get emotional just seeing her in those dresses. I forgot to mention that the bridesmaids will be finding their dresses for the white wedding as well. We have already finalized our traditional engagement dresses for the first day of the wedding. In the Ghanaian American culture, they usually have a traditional African wedding ceremony followed by a white wedding, which is the American styled wedding. Followed by the thanksgiving at the church.

The fact that we all have different schedules makes it hard to meet. So far, everything is going well. Zuhrah found a few dresses. She tried on an Eva Lendel mermaid romantic style lace dress and an off the shoulder sweetheart bell sleeve dress. Zuhrah tried many more, but they weren't memorable enough to remember. She ended up not going with any of them because it didn't feel like the one.

The next place we went to was called Lotus Bridal. She tried on a mermaid dress with detachable sleeves and intricate beading. I was getting emotional just looking at her. Everybody was complimenting her. She tried on two more ivory lace and tulle dresses. Despite this, she wasn't sold on any of the dresses. After that, we went to David's Bridal. To our surprise, there were no dresses she liked there either. We even tried to look for bridesmaids' outfits, but found nothing.

We decided to check a store out called Birdy Grey and found affordable nice dresses for all the bridesmaids and me. The dress we settled upon was a one shoulder in light pink. The color theme of Zuhrah's wedding is pink, gold, and white. Finally, she decided on a dress, which shocked everyone. It was from the bridal shop called New York City Bride. It was so beautiful.

I wish I could say more, but it's supposed to be a surprise. All I can say is it's not a mermaid dress like she wanted, but it's even better. After this long day we all had, it was time to get food. We decided to go to a local restaurant in the area for some Italian food. It was a great time hanging out with them. We shared some laughs and deep conversations.

I knew that I would get along with the bridesmaids because they were a vibe. There was no negative energy amongst the group. We were all here to make Zuhrah's day special and I think we accomplished that.

Three days passed, and I was starting my week by going to work and home. On the fourth day, I get a random text from a 646-area code.

UNKNOWN NUMBER:

Hey, I miss you.

ESI:

Excuse me who's this?

UNKNOWN NUMBER:

So, you really don't know who this is? Let me guess you deleted my number.

ESI:

Nope don't have a clue.

SETH:

Well, it's me, Seth. I miss you.

ESI:

Why are you texting me? I recall you telling me that you aren't the one for me. What's the sudden change?

SETH:

I had a change of heart. I want you back, Esi.

ESI:

I heard you had a new girl after we broke up. I guess things didn't work out with her then. Trouble in paradise huh?

SETH:

What girl? I'm confused?

ESI:

Don't play dumb, someone I know saw you kissing another girl. Why did you come to waste my time?

SETH:

I don't think the person saw me. They might've thought it was me, but it wasn't.

ESI:

Seth, I don't want to argue with you. I know you will never tell me the truth. So please do me a favor delete my number and don't contact me again.

SETH:

You're making a big mistake by saying this.

ESI:

Consider yourself blocked. Bye, have a nice life.

(Number Blocked)

Seth really thought he could come back into my life like nothing ever happened. He assumed I was a fool and would come running back to him. As much as I loved him, I love myself more than anything. Thinking about our interaction is making me angry. I had to block him before I say something I might regret.

The worst thing of it all is that he didn't even apologize for breaking my heart. What he didn't realize was there were many sleepless nights. At times, I thought something was wrong with me. I didn't get the closure I wanted, but at least I spoke up for myself. I didn't allow him to play mind games.

The next few days aren't eventful. I just do my daily routine as usual, but don't feel a sense of enjoyment. I notice that I haven't been keeping up with my appearance lately. All I do is wear my hair in a low bun or afro, which I'm getting tired of. I decide to have a self-care day. I deserve to be happy as well, regardless of what's been going on in my life.

I go to get my bohemian knotless box braids done this morning at a braiding shop in Queens, NY. It's called Queen Mother Braiding Salon. It takes roughly five hours to finish my whole head. I love the hairstyle. I look so beautiful. I feel like an ethereal goddess. The curly pieces in my braids are a nice touch.

Later on, I go to get my nails done. Due to the work I do, I prefer not to get long nails. I feel like it draws too much attention to me. I get short light pink nails. I also get white nail polish on my toenails. It was a nice day pampering myself. When I get to my house, I pull up the Max app on my TV. I scroll through shows to watch and settle on *The Fresh Prince of Bel-Air*.

I am watching the episode where Ashley Banks sings at food court. I was singing along to that song. Every now and again, it's good to go back to what made you happy as a child. This show definitely gave me flashback to times with my siblings watching these kinds of shows. I remember wanting to dress like her and Hilary. Their fashion sense was top notch. It takes me back to times when I didn't have to stress about anything in life.

I'm so lost in watching TV that I forget that I need to eat. As usual, I have to think about what I want. So, I buy myself a Domino's peperoni pizza and brookie dessert. It tastes so good. The flavors captivate my mouth. I'm doing my little happy dance I do when the food is too good.

The rest of the night is spent watching *Euphoria*. I heard about the hype surrounding that show and thought I might give it a try. It's about high school people's lives which involves sensitive topics. I can understand the popularity of it now. The time I go to sleep is extremely late, but thank God it's still the weekend.

The next day, I wake up to a phone call from Zuhrah. She has some exciting news for me and can't contain her joy.

She says, "Hey sis, I want to invite you to the bachelorette trip. Guess where we're going?"

I'm perplexed, thinking, *which country we are traveling to for this trip?* I make my first guess and say, "France?"

She says, "No, silly."

"Then what could it be, because I'm not sure."

She paused for a moment and says, "Esi, we are going to Ghana!!!" Then she says, "Say it with me Esi, yɛwɔ abɔnten." We about to be outside in the next two months. This is exciting, I was wondering when I would have some fun in my life.

"Girl, I have something to tell you," I say.

"What happened? Is everything all right, Esi?"

I tell Zuhrah how Seth texted me and claimed he missed me. As I tell her this, I'm rolling my eyes because this man wasted my time, and I allowed him. I tell her that he wouldn't admit that he was with another woman, so I blocked him.

She says, "Wow, the audacity of him to come back into your life like he didn't break up with you months prior. Ɛyɛ asɛm oo, men really have so much boldness to come pull such nonsense."

I have to agree with her. I couldn't believe he would lie to me even after I had a witness. She's happy that I kicked him to the curb. The journey towards self-love has started. The moment I decided I wanted better for myself is when things changed.

After our conversation, I get ready and do online church. The topic of forgiveness came about. Since it happens to be a bilingual service, the preacher said, "Fa kyɛ wo yɔnko."

The verse is used from Mathew 6:14. It says, "For if you forgive other people when they sin against you, your heavenly father will also forgive you."

Hearing that makes me realize I have to forgive Seth for all the anguish he caused me. I pray for God to take away the hatred in my heart for him. It won't be an easy thing to do. Even though I have forgiven him, I will never forget those emotions. Sometimes it's better to love people from a distance.

A few hours have passed when I get a text from my sister Anastasia. She says that everyone is coming by our parents' home next weekend. This includes my sisters and their spouses and children. We all haven't seen one another for a few months. The thought of us all being together sends my mind into overdrive. Every time we are all together, drama ensues, leaving me wanting to go home.

I have a strange feeling about her text, as if she's up to something. Now that I am single, the comments about me getting a boyfriend won't stop. For all I know, they will try to micromanage my dating life, which is something I don't want. They will begin telling me who I should date and start giving unsolicited advice.

She asks me how I'm doing, which is odd to me because we hardly speak about our lives. I have a better bond with Gabrielle, despite Anastasia and I being closer in age. I always felt that she thought she was better than me. She would try to compete with me in everything. When I fell short in an area of my life, she would rub it in my face.

Anastasia and I don't have the best relationship for that reason and many others. She would always tell my parents things I told her in confidence. I have decided to only tell her things I don't mind getting back to my family. I tell her that my life is going well. She brings it upon herself to ask about what happened between Seth and me.

I'm so uncomfortable by her inquisitive question. I figure my mom is the one that told her. I just tell her that we broke up a few months ago. We just weren't compatible, and it took the breakup for me to come to that conclusion. She wants to pry for more information, but I won't budge.

I don't text her back after that, because there's nothing left to say. I enjoy the rest of my day doing what I love most: relaxing and watching some TV shows. For some, that might be uneventful, but to me, it's the best thing ever. I look forward to times where I just sit and do nothing. I only get this chance every weekend.

At work the next day, I have an IEP meeting to attend. IEP stands for Individualized Education Program. It helps students with disabilities to get services that will help them succeed in school. The meeting I have with other professionals such as teachers, administrators, the school psychologist, and school counselor. The student in question has autism, which has greatly affected their speech. Autism doesn't always impact speech, but in this case it does.

The meeting went well, although it dragged on a bit.

I'm going to my room when I hear my name being called. I turn around and it is Mr. Hensley. I greet him and we walk down the hall. We talk about how our day is going thus far. I tell him that I had an IEP meeting, and he says he just finished teaching a class. He is going to print out class work in the main office.

He's really kind and always cheerful. He is always there to lend an ear when people need it.

I go to my room and say, "See you later, Alligator," to which he responds, "In a while, Crocodile." After that, my day is filled with providing speech therapy to students. I'm exhausted by the time school ends. I barely had time to eat because I had work to do.

My schedule is the same for the whole week. Fast forward to the weekend, and I go to my parents' home in The Bronx. By the time I get there, everyone had arrived. My parents happen to live in Riverdale in a gorgeous neighborhood. They don't have anyone else living with them, so the house is to their liking. The style is a modern concept with gray and white as the theme.

It was around 2pm. I greet everyone one by one to show respect. My mom asks me if I want anything to eat, which is great because I'm starving. My mom made one of my favorite foods, which happens to be waakye. It's a dish that consists of rice and black-eyed peas with stew on top and assorted fried meats. I didn't realize how much I miss home cooked meals. Living alone, I hardly ever cook. Once I finish eating and settle in, the questions on my relationship status start.

I try to avoid the questions, but they keep coming back-to-back. I grow annoyed the more they talk about my love life. I keep thinking, *is anyone concerned about how I feel?* My sisters keep saying that it's not right that my ex broke up with me. They come to an agreement that my ex was wasting my time. I fold my arms across my chest with a forced smile on my face. I can feel myself about to snap. I pretend to have interest in what my family is saying.

It isn't until they mention setting me up with a man that I start listening.

"I have a great guy who I think will be a better match for you, Esi," Gabrielle said. I look at her intently, paying attention to every word. She says his name is Kobby and he is 31 years old. He happens to be a mechanical engineer. According to her, he is interested in getting to know me.

Before I could get a word out, everyone is pressuring me to get in contact with Kobby. Why is everyone so concerned about whether I'll get married in the future? As far as I'm concerned, things happen on God's timing. I tell myself that I won't stress about marriage. My past attempts ended in me being heartbroken. Who's to say this time will be different?

"Esi, will you at least try to talk to Kobby?" my mom says. I don't know what to say. In order to please her, I decide to give it a try. If it doesn't work out, then I can just stop talking to him. After my last relationship, the trust I have for men is dwindling. I want the conversation to be over and for us to talk about something else.

Finally, the attention is off me and onto Anastasia. She is more than excited to tell this news. I wonder what it could be. Anastasia looks at her husband Samson for confirmation.

She has this big smile on her face as she announces to us, "I'm pregnant."

Everyone is cheering, including me, because we know how much it means to her to be a mom. Apart from her dreams in life, she always talked about getting married and starting a family. Her dream came true.

Me, on the other hand, I thought marriage was what I wanted since hitting my late 20s. It turns out that's what I was conditioned to believe because of my family. My main goal now is a blissful life. One that is filled with less stress. I would love to get married one day, but is it my goal in life? No! It took several failed relationships to come to this conclusion.

We all decide it's getting late. One by one, my siblings and I leave the house. I carpool with Gabrielle, her husband, and kid. They have a minivan with eight seats, so there's more than enough room. They bought the van in anticipation of having more kids. I love my niece so much. She is very kind and lights up every room she steps in. Hopefully one day, she'll have more siblings.

A few minutes after I was dropped off, I get a text from Kobby. Although I didn't know it was him until he told me. He knows a bit about me, but wants to know more. Oh no, what has my sister told him about me? I close my eyes and take a deep breath, trying to get myself to calm down. He asks me what I like to do for fun. You know, the basic questions people ask when they're getting to know you.

Once I get comfortable, I ask him why he is single and what happened in his past relationship. He says that his ex would fight all the time and have heated discussions about anything. Someone always seemed to be offended in the end. He realized they had different goals and aspirations. They mutually ended things with one another.

* * *

After this day, I have been talking to this man daily. I can't believe how long we've been speaking to one another for this long. Today makes two weeks. Kobby has been telling me fun facts about himself. He enjoys watching soccer, and his favorite player of all time is Cristiano Ronaldo. It's nice having someone to talk to on a daily basis. I guess I kind of missed having that the past few months. He's pretty funny and goofy, which I like, but I'm still unsure about him. He hasn't asked me out on a date thus far. We've been talking for this long, which is not a lot of time, but it is long enough to at least plan a date. Am I missing something here? So, my suspicions are being amplified. I am probably wasting my time. When I experience moments like this, it's really hard for me to trust anyone.

Regardless, he's not my boyfriend so I can have other option if I choose. I'm not tied down to any man. The problem with that is I prefer to talk to one person at a time. This substantially limits my options when dating. I have to stop thinking that every man I meet is my potential husband. I should go with the flow more and assess the person's nature first. I am a marriage-minded person when I date, but I want to be more carefree and not so strict. During mid-thought, I get a call from my bestie.

"Guess where we're going next weekend, Esi?" Zuhrah says. I'm trying to guess, but she stops me in my tracks and says, "We're going to Atlantic City, New Jersey."

This is such short notice, but not like I was doing something that weekend. A smile forms on my face so wide because I will get to see my bestie again. Plus, this is a great distractor from my thoughts.

"What day and time will we be going on our mini vacation?" I ask her.

She says, "Girl, be ready Friday by 5pm."

I was worried for a second that I wouldn't have time to get ready after work, but I was wrong. Somehow, we start talking about my love life.

"What's going on in your love life?"

"Well, nothing much, other than the fact that I have been talking to this guy named Kobby."

"Really? Tell me more about him."

"My sister Gabrielle told me about him, and she said he's a nice guy who's a mechanical engineer and he's 31 years old."

"Seems like he has his life figured out. We love a man who's ambitious. Do you see it moving into a relationship?"

"Honestly, I am having doubts about him being that we've been talking for two weeks, and he hasn't scheduled a date yet."

"Yeah, something seems very sketchy. I say keep living your best life and if he comes around give him a chance, but date around explore your options. Don't be so rigid."

"You are right about that. I will keep my options open, so I don't get my heart broken. Anyways, how's planning for the wedding going?"

"It's going well, by God's grace, but still stressful being that I have to plan two weddings. The traditional Ghanaian one and the white wedding. The only thing that is helping me is my wedding planner."

"I know it's stressful. If you need anything, please let me know."

"I will, thank you so much, Esi. Don't forget about our trip on Friday, okay?"

"I won't, it will be a fun stress reliever. I will leave you to relax, all right, my friend."

"Okay, bye."

I am so excited to finally be going out with my bestie. She really is a girl's girl, meaning she is a true friend that looks out for my best interest. I don't know what I would have done without her all these years. Just thinking about our friendship gets me emotional. Good friends are hard to come by. I am really blessed to have such an amazing friend. I pray that God helps us to remain friends. As I'm in thought, I get a text message from Kobby.

KOBBY:

Hey Esi, I haven't heard from you all day. Are you all right?

ESI:

Hey there stranger. I can say the same about you. The phone works both ways, you know.

KOBBY:

Dang! What I do. You have a cheeky answer
for me.

ESI:

You are right, I was being a little shady, but I
didn't mean no harm.

KOBBY:

All is forgiven my love. I do have to ask you
something.

ESI:

I'm all ears ask away.

KOBBY:

I would like to take you out on a date
tomorrow night. If that's all right with you.

ESI:

I have been waiting on you to ask, but since
you did, sure, I guess.

KOBBY:

I had to see if we were compatible first before
I asked. You seem like a really cool person to
hang out with, and your sarcasm is top
notch lol.

ESI:

Not to toot my own horn but 😏 Of course I'm
great to be around. You are very lucky my
friend. Lol. Thanks for gassing my head up.

KOBBY:

I gassed you too much, but I mean every
word. Anyways, be ready by 4 pm tomorrow. I
would've said a later time, but I don't want to
keep you out all night. I have something good
in store for you. If you don't mind text, I would
like your address to pick you up.

ESI:

Oooo I'm so excited. Can't wait to see what you have in store. Will send it to you right now. Did you get it?

KOBBY:

Yes, I did. I'm glad you're excited enjoy your day. See you tomorrow.

What are the odds that Kobby wants to go out on a date after I had just been talking about him to Zuhrah? I wonder if my sister has something to do with this. I guess God or some force answered my prayers. He seems like a nice guy, but to wait two weeks to confirm a date is odd. I assume something is up, which is making me have my guard up. Guys tend to hide a lot, but say very little. *God, if this man is wasting my time, let me know. Please give me a sign that shows his true intentions for me.* I might be overreacting, but my heart can't take another heartbreak. It's too much to bear.

Anyways, let me go and be productive. Time for me to finish cleaning my house and get ready to do laundry. It feels like I'm always cleaning nowadays which is a never-ending task. I put on my over-the-ear headphones and put on my 90s playlist. Listening to Tony Braxton has me in a wonderful mood. I'm singing like my rent is due. Lucky for me, I have an in-unit washer and dryer. So long are the days of carrying laundry to the laundromat.

I separate my clothes and begin the process of washing them. In the meantime, while my clothes are being cleaned, I decide to cook. In all honesty, cooking is a drag, but with all these expenses coming up, I can't afford to eat out much. My dinner for the night will be spaghetti and meatballs. It's a quick dinner that will satisfy my hunger and keep me full. I normally don't like eating food that I have to cook. I usually prefer easy meals that take less time. Trust me, I can cook, but laziness is what prevents me from being chef material.

I have to be financially smart if I'm going to maintain my lifestyle. Money has been a sensitive subject for me since I was a child. My parents used to have financial constraints that caused us to live paycheck to paycheck. Living life like that isn't liberating. Always on edge because you're wondering how you will stay afloat. Then you have family back home in Africa asking for money, thinking that money is easily accessible. I vowed to myself that I would never let myself get to that point. I want my future self to be content with my present decisions. It's always good to save for a rainy day.

Can you believe I'm going on a date? What should I wear? What if it's an awkward date? You know some people are better to talk with on the phone versus in person. Am I overthinking this? Why am I so nervous? Earth to Esi, it's not that serious. Just be yourself and let the rest follow. Remember sis, you are the prize and he's lucky to experience a woman like you. Who knows, you might actually enjoy your time. Oh, wait a minute!! I forgot what I will be wearing. *Hmm, let me see what I have.*

As I enter my walk-in closet, I spot the perfect date night outfit. Upon further observation, it's a black button-up tee shirt dress with gold buttons that still has the tags on it. I look up at my shoes and pull out my knee-high dark brown boots and bag to match with gold hardware. To tie it all together, I'm gonna wear gold jewelry. I never go anywhere without my Nefertiti pendant necklace. It's a symbol to me that I'm a queen in my own right. I hear my washer go off, which I happily walk over to and put my clothes into the dryer.

Then I put my second load into the washer. All of a sudden, the sweet sound of Usher's song "You Make Me Wanna" fill the room. I'm jamming to it as if I'm the girl he's talking about. When I get into the musical mood, no one can tell me nothing. *I am the best singer I know*, I tell myself. Now that I got my outfit together, time to eat my dinner. I pray over my food and dig in. I really did my big one with this meal. It tastes so amazing. After I'm finished eating, I clean my dishes and fold my massive pile of laundry. I can't fathom the fact that I wear so many clothes.

I'm growing tired, but instead of sleeping, I spend most of my time ruminating about the date. Normally I don't get nervous, but being out of the dating game has got me a bit out of touch. So many thoughts about what's yet to come, it's driving me insane. I don't know why I care so much about his opinion of me. There's a saying that first impressions matter the most. I want him to like me for me and not who I pretend to be. Not like I'm doing that. The conversations have flowed well, and I feel like myself speaking with him.

Eventually, I fall asleep and wake up the next morning feeling a bit groggy, but nothing a cup of coffee can't fix. I make my coffee just how I like it. Three sugars with caramel drizzle along with French vanilla creamer. By this time, it's at least 12 pm. I decided to eat something quick, a blueberry muffin. It curbs my appetite for the time being while I got ready for my date. Nervousness turned into anxiousness because I want to get the date over with.

I'm not into dating just for the fun of it. Intentionality is what I prefer. At this point, marriage is the end goal. However, I've seen too many instances of people cohabitating for years with no true commitment or ring. It's always one person that convinces the other that marriage isn't necessary. They would get houses, invest in property together, and even have kids, but marriage is where they draw the line? I don't understand. Wish more people thought of the real implications that can happen if a couple never gets married. What if your partner gets sick and you don't have a say in their care because you aren't married?

Although, I'd rather be single than in a horrible marriage that is making me unhappy. This is something I learned long ago from seeing other people's broken marriages. Not only are they miserable, but they give unsolicited bad advice to anyone who will listen. Saying things like, "You must remain married at all costs, because being divorced is a disgrace." I've adopted the new school way of life. I will never let anyone put me through hell and I'd stay. I've spent too much time these past months working on myself that I can't revert back.

Time goes by fast when you're lost in thought. Suddenly, I get a call from Kobby.

"Hey, are you ready for our date in a few?"

"I am almost done, just have to put my shoes on."

"Oh, okay. I will be there in five minutes. Don't keep me waiting too long."

"Ha-ha, very funny. I'll make sure to take my time now."

"There you go again, being sarcastic."

"I can't help it, you started it."

"Whatever do you mean? I have no clue."

"I guess you are giving me a taste of my own medicine huh."

"A little bit."

"Anyways, I will be ready before you come. See you soon."

"All right, see you later."

Using all my force, I pull up my leather boots, zip them up and check myself in the mirror. Then I walk out the door and wait in the lobby. A moment later, I see a grey Mercedes Benz SUV pull up. I look closer to see it's Kobby, which brings a smile to my face. He, in turn, smiles back. As I walk over to the car, I hear music playing from his car. I can't make out the song, but the vibes are there. His car smells and looks so nice, like he just got it detailed.

Let me give you a rundown of Kobby's appearance. He is six feet tall to my knowledge. We'll see if that's true. Men say they're taller than they actually are. Kobby is a brown skinned fella with a full beard that connects. You can tell he cares about his appearance a lot because of his outfit. He has on a white crisp polo with tan pants and loafers to match. He had a nice Cubin link necklace and smelt of intense cologne. I love a man that can dress.

"So, we meet in person." His voice sounds so deep and manly.

"Yes, we finally have. So, are you going to tell where we are going?"

"We are off to an art gallery in the boogey down Bronx!"

"Oh, wow, that's cool."

"I'm glad you like the surprise. Have you ever been to an art gallery?"

"Yes, I have, but it was long ago. When I was in college, I went to the museum of modern art. What about you?"

"This is my first time going to one."

"What made you want to go?"

"I decided to step out of my comfort zone. I hope I like it."

"Well, there's a first time for everything."

"Very true. Can I ask you a question, Esi?"

Ooh he has a question for me; wonder what it could be? He has me feeling so nervous all of a sudden. *Anyways, play it cool, Esi. There's no need to overreact.* "Sure, you can ask me."

"Why are you single? I mean, someone like you shouldn't be."

"That's nice of you, but I have been through a lot with men. Despite this, I've learned to love myself in the process. What about you?"

"I'm sorry you've had bad experiences, but I love how you've been bettering yourself. Well, for me, I had a relationship that wasn't the best. We would fight all the time. I chose my peace in the end."

"Yeah, relationships aren't worth it if you're always fighting."

"Facts."

We arrived at the art gallery after Kobby found parking. It was a short distance from the venue. Soon as we enter, we're greeted by a woman with beautiful ebony skin and fiery red hair, which was perfectly wand-curled. She wears a black crop top from Diesel and cargo pants with designs. She welcomed us to the gallery. One thing I noticed about the exhibition is that it has art from people of color. I'm not well-versed in art. I can't recognize the names. Each art piece is different than the previous one. This sparks more conversation between us.

"So, what artists from the exhibition have you heard of before coming here?"

"To be honest, Esi, I haven't heard of any prior to coming here."

"Same, but these art pieces are marvelous. I mean, wow, I'm lost for words."

"Likewise, seeing their work being displayed makes me elated. I love seeing people of color excel in their passions."

"Me too, I have a newfound appreciation for art. What artist have you heard of in general?"

"School has always taught about the well-renown ones. One I can think of is Vincent Van Gogh."

"Wasn't he the one that made *Starry Night*?"

"Esi, yes, he's the one."

"I guess we know more about art than we think."

"You are right about that."

The conversation was flowing nicely. Two intellectual minds joined together is a force to be reconned with. This man is well versed. Even though we don't know too much, about art it was good speaking on what we do know. Education is very important to me. It doesn't always have to be formal, but I believe everyone should educate themselves. No one knows it all. Before you became an expert, you were once a student learning and grasping information. Kobby is my kind of person. We talk until we get hungry. We spent approximately two hours looking at art and engaging in discussion.

"Hey, since we're in the area, why don't we eat here and I'll drive you back home. Sounds like a plan?"

"Sure, I'm never going to turn down food. Ha-ha, a girl's got to eat."

He chuckles a bit before continuing his thought. "There's this place I've went to called Yopcity. You know, the spot that serves West African dishes."

"I actually think I know what you're talking about. Me and my home girl been wanting to go there."

"Today's your lucky night, then."

"I guess it is," I say with a smile.

In the car, music is blasting, leaving me in a daze. This date appears to be running smoothly. Although, this date has made me realize the importance of going out more and living life. Beginning to understand the phrase "Que sera sera." It means whatever will be, will be. I won't force the situation with Kobby, I will just let it flow. If it works out, fine; if not, that's all right. I've kind of gotten used to disappointment so much that I don't even care about the outcome of tonight.

We arrive at the location, but due to parking issues, it takes a while to get inside the restaurant. Finally, someone moves out of their parking spot, which is great for us. We sit down in the restaurant, being greeted by the server. He asks us what we would like to eat from the menu. I glance over it before deciding on dibi. This is a Senegalese dish which consists of seasoned grilled meat such as lamb, including rice, onions, and mustard sauce. The thought of eating this in a few is sending me over the moon.

Kobby, on the other hand, chooses attieke with lamb as his choice of meat. We both get a bottle of orange Fanta. You know, the one straight from Africa. The waiter leaves to start our order.

"So Esi, what do you like most about your job?"

"I like the ability to make an impact on the lives of children with a range of speech problems."

"Wow, that's amazing that you are passionate about what you do. Love that."

"Why thank you. If you don't love what you do, you'll be miserable."

"Totally agree, that's why I didn't listen to people telling me which career path to choose."

"I don't like it when people impose their believes or vision for your life."

"Me neither, it's like they want to live vicariously through you. So they don't have to worry about their own life."

"That is a word."

We are so deep in conversation it doesn't even occur to us that our food arrived.

"I guess we should dig in," I say with a smile.

"Yes, we should. Have you ever tried dibi?"

"No, it's my first time, but I heard it was delicious."

"It's always nice to try new things. I had dibi before and all I can say is, believe the hype."

I start eating my food and I'm impressed. The flavors are there, and you can tell whoever made the meal did it with love. "This meal is so delightful. I'm savoring every moment," I say.

"That's how I felt when I tried this for the first time."

"How about you, like your meal?"

"Absolutely, this is wonderful."

Time passes and we finish eating our food. Like a gentleman, he is trying to pay for the meal. I don't even think to offer because if a man wants to do something nice, you let them. We walk to his car, and he drives me back to my apartment.

"It was nice getting to meet the person I've been talking to."

"Likewise," I say with a nervous chuckle.

"Thank you for allowing it to be a good date. I was nervous for a second."

"Nervous? For what?"

"I was nervous that you were a catfish."

"What about me screams catfish?"

"I never said you were, just nervous you could be. I've had past experiences with women."

"Well, I'm no catfish, one-hundred-percent natural beauty over here."

"Sorry if I offended you, it wasn't my intention."

"Apology accepted."

"Have a good night, talk to you soon."

"Thank you for a great date. Talk to you later. Let me know when you get home."

Chapter Three

AND WE MOVE...

GABRIELLE, ONE OF THE CLOSEST PEOPLE TO ME, IS VISITING ME IN Queens. "Our first date was the last time I heard from Kobby, Gabrielle."

She has a perplexed look on her face. "Wow, what a jerk. Men!" she says, shaking her head. "He didn't tell you why he ghosted you?"

"Actually, no he didn't. I just woke up the next morning and found out I was blocked. Called from a Google voice number and was told never to call him again."

"Ei! Ei! I can't fathom he would do this. I'm so sorry. I thought I should tell you the reason why. At least it might give you some type of closure."

"You introduced him to me, that's the least you can do," I say in a snappy tone. "I am so tired of men, it's so exhausting dealing with them."

"Ouch, that one hurt. I get it, you are hurt. So, the reason he did all this was because he is set to marry someone this weekend. His fiancée threatened to tell his parents and their families if he didn't stop talking to you."

"He legit didn't have to put me through this. For what? Am I a bad person, Gabrielle?" I could feel tears forming in my eyes. I just let out a sigh.

"You aren't a bad person, Esi. Dating is hard. It's filled with broken people that haven't taken the time to heal." She leans over, rubbing my back with a concerned look on her face.

So many thoughts I'm experiencing in this moment. Kobby could've left me alone and not inquire about me. Then I wouldn't be feeling like this. Fiancée! He had a whole fiancé. Wow, wonders shall never end.

"I've decided to decenter men from my life. I think it's the best decision, being that I've had a bad streak with the male species."

"Don't say that."

"What do you mean, don't say that? You don't know how it feels to be single or to have failed interactions with men. You have a man. You can only imagine how I feel, you don't experience my reality."

"Again, I'm sorry."

"So, you're telling me he's set to marry. How do you know?"

"I heard through a mutual friend who was invited to the traditional and white wedding. He didn't invite me, knowing I'd never introduce you to him."

"Well, the damage is already done and now I know how to move accordingly."

"Take all the time you need to heal. I wish I never allowed you to meet him."

"Okay what do you want me to say? I forgive you? Right now, I'm upset, so please just..." I let out another sigh, lowering my head into my hands, and stop my thought midsentence.

She just stands there with nothing more to say. Shortly after, my sister leaves. The apartment is so quiet, I need something to fill the room, but I can't bring myself to put on music or a TV show. I just lay there in bed letting my mind consume me. Looking around at all the uplifting images of black joy in my room was the opposite of my current state. My eyes land on the portrait of myself smiling back when I felt my most confident. Shaking my head is all I can do. It has been a few days since he ghosted me and while I shouldn't care, I can't help but be perturbed. Bothered by the fact that yet again, my belief on love was confirmed. What happens for others may never be my fate, and I have to be content with that. I remember in that second about the trip to Atlantic City with Zuhrah. This is going to be the best distractor from this situation.

Girl, you better not cry! Don't shed not one tear! Especially not over some cowardice punk. Someone that didn't have the common decency to tell the truth. If only I didn't wear my heart on my sleeve. I wouldn't attract these kinds of people. These types of people prey on the vulnerable, leaving you broken and seeking answers you'll never get. So, is the ex he talked about his fiancée, or might I add, soon-to-be wife? Why would she agree to marry a cheat? If he could do it once, he'll do it again. He's a walking red flag and will only be a terrible partner. *Esi, snap out of it! You're not in this situation anymore for a reason. We move...*

My thoughts about the situation are loud. I'm mad at my sister for getting me involved with Kobby. She seems apologetic, but that doesn't negate the fact that my time was wasted. Mad is an understatement. I'm livid with Kobby for thinking he'd get away with cheating. I mean, he did and wasn't held accountable. The concept of being worthy of love makes me conflicted. My mind says I'm worthy of adoration, but my heart knows I'm lying. Time after time, I get let down after having my hopes up. Let me go to sleep. At least it'll make this feeling more bearable.

Two days pass. It's the day I have been anticipating. It's my mini staycation with Zuhrah. Yay! I make sure to pack everything that will be needed. I'm usually an over-packer, but today is better. After work, I go straight to Zuhrah's house. Work was busy as usual, and because of this, time went by fast.

"Esi, how are you?" She gives me a warm embrace, which makes me shed a tear. I guess her inquiring about my feelings struck something inside.

With tears in my eyes and a brittle voice, I say, "It's been a challenging few days. I found out that Kobby is getting married this weekend."

"What!? Awurade Nyame. I'm so sorry, you don't deserve this. How did you find out?"

"My sister Gabrielle told me. The dating pool has been treacherous. Filled with flawed humans who refuse to work on themselves and keep hurting others. I told myself I wouldn't cry, but I'm hurt—not because I loved him or anything. It's the lie that pains me. He blocked me and when I called from a different number, he said never to contact him again."

She looks me in my eyes and says these words. "Your feelings are valid. The reason he lied shows he didn't have regard for you. The audacity of him to do that to you should fuel you to better yourself. You're worthy of a love that isn't deceitful and doesn't make you question who God destined you to be. I know I shouldn't tell you what to do, being that I'm not in your situation. I want to see you shine. Just know this weekend, we are going to enjoy ourselves."

Her smile and watching her speak with such assurance makes me feel okay.

"I appreciate your words. I know what you're saying isn't with any malice. I will get over this eventually. However, I'm not interested in dating anymore. Love shouldn't hurt this bad. From Seth to Kobby, I don't know who is worse. I'm deserving of all life's greatest blessings, but why don't I believe that with love?"

"Someone's inability to love you doesn't change what God says about you. You might not realize it now, but you will. I'm sending you lots of love and praying you don't give up on it."

I have nothing left to say. Something in me changes in this moment. I'm through fighting for what's not meant for me. Done having to build myself back up after disappointment. Tired of the way things are going. If only God could remove this feeling of wanting to be chosen. I've learned that fairytales lied about having a happily ever after. Made it seem like the right guy would eventually sweep you off your feet. He would be your prince charming. While that's true for some, this story line doesn't apply to the masses.

"Earth to Esi. Let's go and have some fun."

Forcing a smile when I'm hurting is the most strenuous thing.

"All right, Zuhrah, let's go!"

Zuhrah drives us to Atlantic City, New Jersey, which is a good ride. She plays our favorite songs along the way. We arrive at the Hard Rock Hotel and check into our rooms at the front desk. As we roll our luggage to the elevator, we're marveling at the scenery. I'm happy that I get to relax after having a difficult week. The hotel suite is very nice and pristine. I saw the TV has Zuhrah's name on the screen. The bathroom is my favorite because I can take nice selfies.

"Zuhrah, what are we doing tonight?"

"We are going to the Sugar Factory! It's in the hotel, so it won't be a hassle to travel."

"All right, sounds good. I actually haven't been there before. So, this shall be interesting. I was told their drinks are unique."

"Same, I heard that too."

We get settled in the room and talk about our aspirations. Outside of my love life woes, I'm doing pretty well for myself. Thinking about it, I'm blessed to have the life I live. However, I want a better future, one that I can make an impact.

"Esi, it's time for us to get ready. I made a reservation for 9 pm."

"You ain't got to tell me twice. I'm getting ready now."

"Which outfit should I wear?" She picks up two options, and I point to the brown, collared, button-down halter top. She picks some bell-bottom jeans to go with it.

"Thanks for the help. I'm going to do my makeup."

Now it's time for me to pick my outfit. Sifting through my luggage isn't bad. I find a square neckline mocha dress that was flowy. As usual, I have some gold accessories.

My makeup is simple but cute. I usually don't wear heavy makeup. It's not my style. Zuhrah does a neutral look that has me in awe. We put on our outfits and take some photos once we got to the Sugar Factory. We're greeted by the hostess and directed to our seats once we finish our mini photo shoot. The wait time wasn't long because of the reservation.

"Esi, what would you like to eat and drink? I'm thinking of getting a burger."

"Hmmm. I don't know what to get, there's so many options. The cajun chicken penne alfredo looks nice."

"You're right, there's so many options. Especially for the drinks. I'm definitely getting the waffle breakfast burger."

"Let me see the drink selection too. I think you might be on to something."

We both gasped when we saw the selection of milkshakes.

"Zuhrah, I think I will get the princess make-a-wish because it's pinktastic!" I say with a chuckle. We laugh after that.

"Don't you feel better now? I know this is a temporary solution to what you're experiencing. Just know I'm your friend and I want what's best for you."

"I needed that laugh it felt good to not be upset. Men are really draining and have disappointed me for far too long. It's time for me to focus my energy into my interests."

"Men can really do that to you, but I pray you find the most amazing man for you. One that is God-fearing, generous with his heart and kind. Someone that will remind you of God's love."

"Thank you, from your lips to God's ears." Although I want to believe Zuhrah's words over my romantic life, I can't because of all that I've been through. Can't say I'm the happiest with God right now. Why allow me to have the desire of love if I'm never going to experience it? Well, let me not say *never*, because life changes unexpectedly.

We get served our food, and instead of getting a milkshake like we discussed, Zuhrah gets a Virginia strawberry lemonade drink. In her words, "I wanted to spice things up and get something with a little sweet treat."

"I have to ask, how's wedding planning going for you?"

"It's a bit stressful, but I'm grateful to have help from my wedding planner. She has been the best help. Also, I have you as my maid of honor. I didn't want to overwhelm you with tasks to do for the wedding. Since we will be off to Ghana in the summer for two weeks. We will have so much to do there before the two main weddings. I am also in need of a dress for my court wedding."

"I'm so excited for our girl's trip to Ghana. I can definitely help you find a nice dress for your court wedding. We'll be in Ghana, I'm sure you'll find something nice by great designers."

"You're right about that, Esi."

We continue to eat our food in silence for a few minutes. "How are you liking your food and the pinktastic milkshake you got?"

"Very good, it's just so much for me to drink. I'm already full. What about you?"

"It's all so good I can't help myself. The drink is my favorite."

A while after, our waiter asks how we're enjoying ourselves. By the time she comes over, we're done with our meal and are requesting our bill. Zuhrah wants to pay, but knowing her expenses for the wedding, I feel bad. So, I suggest we split the bill and add a tip. We're back to our room after that. I'm so exhausted that I keep yawning as we're walking. I guess it's a sign I'm getting old. I'm not the party animal anymore.

"Esi, what is a dream you have for yourself?"

I take in a deep sigh. "My dream is to be truly content with whatever situation life throws my way. I want to be successful in everything I do and make more money to live extremely comfortably."

"I agree with you, but I also want to add that I want a happy and God-centered marriage for myself and that for all my friends and family."

I keep quiet and just listen. I know that even though I might not believe in love now, who knows where life will take me.

"I think you will meet a remarkable person that will make you forget about all the men before. Please don't give up on love, my friend."

I love that she believes I'll find the relationship of my dreams. I've been hurt so bad that the only thing that will make me content is to focus on myself. I'm tired.

All I can say is, "Amen, I receive it." A question is itching in my mind. "Zuhrah, what would you think life would be like for you if you weren't getting married?"

"I guess I would focus on my passions more. You know I always had a knack for writing. I would write poetry and publish it for the world to read. I would work on my public speaking so I could be on TED Talk."

"What is stopping you from doing that now?"

"You know when you get married, two separate people become one joined in union. My life becomes intertwined with that of my partner, Tobenna. I want him to join in on my future plans."

"Oh, I see." Eventually the room grows silent, and I realize she's fast asleep.

I wish Zuhrah the best in her marriage and pray she'll have a fruitful one that won't end in divorce. We cast out any plans from the enemy to destroy their union. This night, I am reassured that I will be all right with or without a significant other. Peace comes over me that beats all understanding. I sleep so well that when the next morning comes, I'm well-rested. Zuhrah is still fast asleep. I decide to get ready for the day. I put on a nice flowy dress and go bare face. Zuhrah wakes up and immediately smiles at me.

"Girl, you look good. Why didn't you wake me up sooner?"

"Thank you sis, and I didn't want to wake you up in case you were still tired."

"Vacations aren't meant for sleeping."

"What? Best believe after working so hard we better find time to relax and sleep."

"You right about that."

Zuhrah finishes getting ready before she tells me what we'll be doing for the day. "Guess where we are headed."

"You know I suck at making predictions, but if I had to guess, are we going for brunch?"

"Good try, but no. We're actually going to the spa and then we can order room service. What do you think about that?"

"Wow, that's nice. I'm ready to be pampered. Let's go!"

Zuhrah and I walk over to the spa. When we arrive, the ambiance is amazing. It has a warm and cozy environment. We request a deep tissue massage that releases chronic pain and muscle tension. We're taken into a room to change into robes. Then we're escorted into the massage area. The whole fifty minutes, we don't speak to one another. The masseuse targets every pressure point in my body. It's a great time. After we're done, we go back to the hotel and order room service.

We order some food, which includes Belgian waffles with maple syrup and mixed berries, vanilla-cinnamon French toast, two eggs, breakfast potatoes, and bacon. We can't forget the drinks, so we both get cranberry juice. The food didn't come until approximately forty-five minutes later. I really enjoyed eating and relaxing to the sound of music playing in the background. Before you knew it, we had already finished our brunch. It's great, just relaxing with my friend. I never knew this is what I need after experiencing yet another disappointment.

"Sis, how is the trip planning to Ghana going? I mean, the trip is three months away."

"It's actually going okay, but I need some of the girls to communicate better, because since announcing the trip to them, I haven't gotten an update. I will be reaching out to everyone to see what's going on."

"If none of them show up, you know I will."

"Thanks, Esi. I know I can count on you to have a good time with."

"No problem, you know it will be an amazing experience. Who would dare pass it up."

"I know, right! The main issue is, I don't think some of the girls have their visas and time is ticking."

"Oh yeah, having a visa is the most important thing. You can't even enter Ghana without a visa. I hope the girls get it together so we can have an enjoyable time."

Zuhrah just nods her head in agreement.

"I am totally understanding, Esi, so even if they can't come, I won't be offended. I just want us to have fun since we work all the time, and I don't see them often."

"That's very true, we are adulting and part of that is working. Although I love what I do, I get exhausted after the week is over, which makes me not want to do much but stay home. Thank you so much for inviting me to Atlantic City. I really needed this, for real. I love you, sis."

She gives me a big hug and says, "You deserve to have a life of luxury and leisure to do whatever you want. You deserve true happiness that exist beyond borders. So fulfilling that you smile randomly because life has been so good to you. I'm glad I could make you feel better. You have a confidant in me."

We randomly decide to go to the indoor pool in our hotel and just check the scenery out. Luckily for us, the pool area isn't packed, and we have time to sit and relax. What would've made the experience more soothing was to have a book and some slow music. Zuhrah and I just chat about ways we could improve our life with actionable steps. I love having a friend that can have deep conversations and bounce ideas. We swim for a little while as well and even race each other. I'm so glad I talked her into doing swimming lessons when we were twenty. It was a great decision because swimming is a useful life-saving skill depending on the situation. There are so many people who don't know how to swim and never learn.

Zuhrah made a good point that we should always prepare ourselves for anything life throws at us. Who knows, you might be able to save a life. After swimming, we take some amazing selfies and full body pictures for our Instagrams. To her surprise, she gets so many likes and so do I. I think it's because we're giving body, and our face cards are eating. Some men I haven't talked to in years comment under my post, but I pay it no mind. I just look at the comments and laugh with my bestie. The next thing on the agenda is to find a nightclub to go to have some fun. Let's see if she will agree to it, being that we're both grannies at the core of us.

"Hey girl, we should do something fun for our last night here. What do you say about going to a nightclub? It would be fun," I say in a sing-song kind of way.

"Sis, I was hoping you would ask. Didn't want to overstep since I know partying isn't neither of our thing."

"I know, but I say let's enjoy ourselves. Tomorrow is back to reality."

"That true. The question I have is, where are we going?"

"Let me see. Well, there's one at the hotel. I remember the receptionist telling us about this place called The Balcony. We should go there, I mean it's walking distance. So, we can easily leave when we want."

"Good idea, let's get ready."

We walk back to our room and then begin getting dolled up for the night. I'm so excited that I do a whole face beat, which I normally never do. I'm doing a double take in the mirror like, *who is she?* She is me.

"That is what I'm talking about Esi, you're looking tantalizing."

"Aww thanks, and you're stunning as well."

"Let's hurry up and get dressed. So, the fun can begin."

"You're right, let's go. It's already 11pm."

We head over to the club. It's nearly full, but we don't let that stop us from having a good time. The music is blasting, and we are just dancing to the sounds. After about an hour, Zuhrah gets approached by a tall dark-skinned man about 6 feet 3 inches tall, who has a slim muscular frame. He has on a diamond chain that glistens as he approaches us. The whole time he keeps glancing at me, but I don't know much about him. Here is how the conversation goes between the both of them.

"Hey Zuhrah, I knew I saw you when you first came in, but I wasn't sure it was you until I went to get a drink. What are you doing here and without Tobenna? Is this a girl's night out?"

"OMG, is that Amadi in the flesh? I cannot believe my eyes. I haven't seen you in so long. To answer your question, my friend over here, Esi, decided we should go on a girl's night out, which I agreed."

Zuhrah introduces us to one another. I say hi to him and shake his hand. He is very nice, which is refreshing, but every guy is nice in the beginning. So, nothing special.

"Cool, cool. If you want to hang out with my friends, we've got a section."

She looks at me and asks if I want to join them and I reply with, "Sure."

We follow him to the booth with his friends, and he introduces us. I'm not going to lie, I completely forget their names but one thing about me: I never forget a face.

After a few minutes, when liquid courage starts to kick in for

Amadi, he strikes up a conversation. "You look so gorgeous, Esi. I hope I am not overstepping my boundaries. I'm assuming you have a man."

Oh boy, here we go again with men giving compliments and wanting to make a pass at me. "Thank you so much. I'm single to say the least."

"Such a ravaging beauty like yourself is single, wow."

"Life happens and being single doesn't take away from my attractiveness."

"I didn't mean to offend you, just assumed that you were taken already."

"Nope, I'm not, and it's a long story I prefer not to get into right now." The whole time, Amadi is looking at me intently like he cares what I have to say.

"I'm in the same boat, but I understand. So, are you a part of the wedding?"

"Yes, I'm the maid of honor. I think you are in it as well, right?"

"You're right, I am the best man. I'm so happy for Tobenna. He really found an amazing woman."

"Of course she is. They are lucky to have found each other."

He pauses for a second, not knowing what to say next. I assume he's nervous, but to my surprise, he isn't.

"I find it funny that Zuhrah is at the club. We could never get her to go back in college."

"You went to Stonybrook for undergrad? I never saw you. What a small world."

"Yeah, me neither. I was either studying or partying. I would've recalled seeing you because my memory is good."

I then pull Zuhrah over, who is jamming to the music, in a daze to tell her this newfound revelation.

"Hey, you never told me that Amadi went to school with us."

"Oh, I definitely forgot. He is a year older than us, so maybe that's why you never saw him. Plus, he's into accounting and you chose psychology. So, it's nearly impossible for you two to cross paths. Not to mention you were into your books and never left your apartment."

"True, true, but dang, you ain't gotta air me out like that."

"Sorry, I love you girl. Didn't mean to."

Amadi laughs and says, "Wow, love your friendship with one another."

I reply with, "That's my girl. She's a loyal friend and I care about her. Even with her antics. I'm down for the ride."

"Good friends are so hard to come by. So glad you have each other."

"Me too. So, what are the odds we see you at the club?"

He clears his throat to say, "Me and my homeboys decided to have fun tonight. It's been a rough week for us all."

Who you telling. I just nod in agreement because I don't feel like disclosing my relationship woes. The music selection blows me away. At some point I'm singing along with Zuhrah. The beats and melody of music gets me in the mood. It was around 1 am by this time, and ya girl is tired. I nudge Zuhrah to leave.

She doesn't object because homegirl is yawning every five seconds. We say goodbye to the guys before leaving. I can tell Amadi doesn't want us to leave.

"Have a good night, ladies. Do you need a ride?"

"I appreciate your kind gesture, but we have a room at the hotel. We will be fine," I say.

"Oh, okay, stay safe. See you around." On our way to our room Zuhrah strikes up a conversation.

"Girl, I know it's too soon and you probably don't want to hear this, but Amadi likes you."

"I figured as much, but I'm trying to focus on other things. Relationships have had me in distress and quite frankly, I'm tired."

"I think you should focus on your healing journey and then if it's meant to be, he'll understand. I want the best for you."

"Yes, my healing is important to me right now."

Everyone wants love, but only few ever experience true love that doesn't take account of wrongs. That doesn't hurt so bad you question your worth. I believe that both people need to be deeply invested for any relationship to work. They also have to be willing to make sacrifices for one another. The idea of love scares me because of the liars and cheaters that come into your life with nothing to offer but broken promises. I keep this thought to myself. As much as I want to love, I'm emotionally downcast. However, I know this feeling won't last long due to my resilient nature. Once we reach our room, I get my comfy clothes, take off my makeup, do my skincare, and fall asleep. All in that order. Zuhrah knocked out as soon as she wiped her face.

I wake up early next morning. You can say it's my body's internal clock. Check out was at 11am. I never understand why hotels don't have later times. It's 10 am, and we both have gotten ready to leave. After we check out, we're hungry. I suggested we find a nice brunch spot once, which made Zuhrah excited. We find this place called Lola's Café and have the time of our lives. I eat French toast, eggs, bacon, and a mimosa. Zuhrah has buttermilk pancakes, eggs, sausage, and an apple juice. We love our meals and give a nice tip to the server, who was attentive the whole time.

After our meal, it's time to snap back into reality. On our way back to my apartment, I'm in deep thought. I'm no longer sad about Kobby, being that he was never my boyfriend. I'm disappointed because I had my high hopes for a man that lied. I know I will overcome this, but I will never forget him and the men before. They have all taught me lessons I will always remember. Love yourself first, because humans' feelings for you are fleeting.

"Esi, why have you gotten so quiet? You all right, girl?"

"I'm all right, just thinking."

"Don't think too hard. We have arrived at your apartment."

"Okay. I can't believe we're here already. Thank you so much for the trip and your friendship."

"Esi, you are my dearest friend. I'd do anything to make you happy, and you know that. See you later, and don't think about that person anymore."

"How'd you know?"

"I guess you can call it intuition."

"I won't, and see you around. Get home safe and text me if you need anything."

"Will do."

Chapter Four

COULDN'T HAVE EXPECTED THIS...

I'VE BEEN MINDLESSLY SCROLLING ON MY PHONE FOR THE PAST thirty minutes when I get a follow request on Instagram. I look closely at the account and notice the profile picture is Amadi from a few weeks back. The first question that comes to mind is, *how did he find me?* I assume he found me through Zuhrah's page because we are mutuals. He was cool and easy to talk to, so I hit the confirm button. He didn't give me the ick. As soon as I do, I get a bunch of likes on my pictures, followed by a message.

AMADI:

Hey Esi, how are you?

ESI:

Fine I guess, just preparing for the girl's trip to Ghana in two weeks and my sister's baby shower next week on Saturday.

AMADI:

That's what sup, a trip to the motherland is always nice. Looks like you got a lot to prepare for. But why you planning so early for your trip?

ESI:

Yes, it is, and the reason is so I can make sure I have everything I need. I hate waiting till the last minute. You're right, I do have a lot on my plate smh.

AMADI:

Gotcha makes sense. I'm guessing you are an over packer. Right?

ESI:

If you call being prepared means that I'm an over packer, then I guess I am lol. How have you been?

AMADI:

I have been all right, nothing too much has been happening in my life. I wanted to ask you something if you don't mind.

ESI:

Oh, okay. I wonder what's the question you have in mind?

AMADI:

You seem like an amazing person. I would like to get to know you better over some dinner or even lunch. If that's okay with you.

ESI:

Thank you for the offer, but I would like for this outing to be on a friends' basis. I have my reservations about this, which has nothing to do with you personally. Just been through a lot and want to take the pressure off things.

AMADI:

I totally get it. We can go as friends. What do you have in mind for our first meet up? Would you mind us meeting up tomorrow?

ESI:

I like something fun, like arcade games, sort of like Dave and Busters. I'm a foodie at heart. Wherever there's food, count me in. Since tomorrow is Saturday and I have nothing planned, we can meet up.

AMADI:

Okay I hear you loud and clear. How about we go to Gaming City which is an arcade place in Queens? I can pick you up around 3 pm. Then we can eat at a Korean BBQ restaurant.

ESI:

That would be great, and I live in Queens so that's convenient for me. Korean BBQ seems like it would be tasty. Legit haven't been to one but there's a first for everything.

AMADI:

All right sounds like a plan. I look forward to seeing you tomorrow.

ESI:

Me too. Talk to you later.

Something tells me this man wants to be more than friends. Should I go along with this outing or call it off? I have been through so much. I want to take away the pressure of finding the one and let happiness lead the way. He seems so nice, I don't want to hurt his feelings by not going. *What are you thinking, Esi? If you don't go, you'll miss out on having fun and getting to know Amadi. Plus, you are both in the wedding, might as well get acquainted now. All right girl, you're going, and it will be fun regardless of the outcome,* I say to myself. I need to figure out what I will wear. I opt for something casual, so as to not be too dressed up.

I continue packing up my luggage. I have so many cute outfits that I can't wait to wear for Ghana. This experience is much needed, and wonderful things are going to come about. I'm smiling because I know God is in control of my situation. A while later, I am finished packing. I realize that I did not wrap the presents for Anastasia's baby shower next week. I got her baby gender neutral clothing, being that we still don't know the sex of the child. My sister legit wants to wait until the shower to reveal the news to us. The only person that knows is my mom. I'm surprised she hasn't given hints because this lady is a blabber mouth. My mom is a social butterfly, so naturally, we thought she'd spill the secret. She is proving us all wrong.

I'm in awe of the items I got my niece or nephew. I even got Anastasia a gift too, because she's the one bringing life. I got her stuff to help with recovery. At times, people often neglect the mom and focus on the baby. I can go on and on about this topic. I put my wrapping skills to use, which makes me proud. Time passes and I'm growing tired. Naturally, I fall asleep and wake up at around 9:30 am. I listen to worship music and pray before getting ready for the day. I see my phone flash, and I notice it's a message from Amadi. He wants to know if we are still meeting today. I confirm that I'm coming. He'll pick me up at 3 pm like we had planned. I eat a light breakfast that consists of a fruit parfait with granola.

Time passes so quickly when you are occupied. Before I know it, it's time to head downstairs to meet Amadi. He drives a gray Toyota Highlander hybrid. It's nice that he got out of his car to greet me and open the door for me. His car is clean and smelled nice. Similar to Kobby's car, but much nicer inside. Of course, he has the little Nigerian flag on his dashboard.

"Are you excited for our day of fun?" Amadi asks.

"Yes, I am. I have never been to a Korean BBQ. So, this shall be interesting."

"That makes two of us, because I haven't either. Going out for food is my favorite pass-time."

"Boy, who you telling? I love food."

"I'm glad we share that in common." We talk so much that I didn't notice we arrived at Gaming City.

"We're here!! You ready to enter?"

"You bet I am. Let's go!" I have this enthusiasm about me. Like I already know it will be a good day. We enter the facility and go to the front desk to get tokens. Amadi pays for them since, in his words, the entire day out is his treat.

"Do you want to go to the dancing grid?" I suggest.

"Yes, then after we can try our luck at the claw machine. That's if you're up for it?"

"Sounds like a plan to me." As I start playing the game, I notice that my dance moves are being put to the test. The floor lights up and I do my best. With each move, I'm remembering my early days in dance class during elementary school. My mom always made sure my sisters and I were enrolled in extracurricular activities. In this moment, I am thanking her.

"Wow, you are so amazing at this game. I wonder if you've ever taken classes for this. I can barely keep up."

Flashing him a smile, I say, "Something like that, I guess." After that I'm tired, but it was fun. We walk over to the claw machines. "Are you any good at these, Amadi?"

"Nah, but for you I can put my skills to the test," he says with a nervous chuckle.

He tries his luck at the machine with the stuffed animals inside. When I tell you he tried his best to get me one of those animals. He fails, but that's okay because the thought behind it is enough for me. I also try and I would've gotten a prize too, but the claw drops the item as it's moving, and I decide to not try again.

Amadi and I walk over to the classic arcade games. That was my favorite. "I bet I can beat you in this racing game."

"You sure about that, Esi?" We both get into this competitive mode. I pout a little because we tie at the end.

"Are you upset?"

"Kind of, but I'll get over it." We even play basketball. Now I know I am not good at sports, but I can't let him know that. With all my might, I'm dunking the ball into the basket. He is as well, but he wins.

Instead of being obnoxious about winning, he says, "Well done, you did amazing. Did you have fun? I surely did."

"Yeah, I most certainly enjoyed myself." We play more games for another hour before heading to the Korean BBQ. I'm thrilled with excitement; it rubs off on Amadi.

"Since neither of us have been to a restaurant like this, I wonder how it will be like, Esi."

"I'm sure it will be great." We enter the facility and get a table for two. We were not aware that we have to cook our own food. We both look at each other in astonishment.

"What are you getting Amadi? I am probably going to eat the spicy pork bulgogi with white rice, peppers, and onions. For my drink, I'll get the strawberry lemonade."

"Thanks for asking. I want the spicy pork belly and spicy chicken bulgogi with white rice, pepper, onion, and mushroom. For my drink, hmm, I have been eyeing the peach lemonade. So that's what I'm considering."

"Oh, okay, that sounds delicious. I cannot wait to dig in."

Sooner than we thought, the food comes and we both get ready to put the meats on the grill.

"I know a thing or two about grilling," Amadi says.

"Me too, my dad taught me so well. I remember those family events we used to have and being near my dad while he grilled."

"Cool."

The food comes out perfectly. Amadi even shares some of his chicken bulgogi with me and it's so mouthwatering. The flavors captivate my tongue. By the time I knew it, it's getting late. We talked and shared some laughs. It was an amazing time spent with him. He pays for the whole meal, which is gentlemanly of him to do.

"Are you ready to go home?"

"Yes, I am. Thanks for taking me out. I really enjoyed my time with you."

"It's my treat. I am glad things worked out today, it was the most fun I've had in a long time. Thank you for that."

With a nervous laugh, I say, "No problem."

Amadi drives to my apartment, but for some reason I don't want to get out the car. So, I stay, and we just talk. I know from this day on, things won't go back to normal. Something is different about this guy that sets him apart from the rest. He listens to me and shares banter.

We both are stunned by how much we talk. It's 11 pm and I'm growing weary. So, we call it a night.

"You are great woman. I hope you know that."

"Thank you. Have a good night and get home safe. Text me when you arrive."

"Will do. Have a great night."

He knows how to make me forget about the things troubling me. How refreshing it is to meet him at the time I did. It's like God places people in your life at the time you need them the most. I keep this meeting a secret from my family and friends, knowing that if things turn sour between Amadi and me, I don't have to go through telling them the news. Amadi would text me daily after that day. We FaceTime for hours and sleep on the phone together. I feel like a kid again.

Saturday is the baby shower for Anastasia. The theme is all white. I could've brought a plus one, but Amadi isn't my boyfriend. So, I don't want to give the wrong impression. I start to get ready, putting my makeup on and styling my hair that was dark brown with honey blonde highlights. I put in some wand curls. The outfit I am wearing is a v-cut dress with fringe at the bottom. It looks nice against my hourglass frame. As someone who is almost two hundred pounds and has a curvy shape, it is difficult to find clothes that are modest. I'm taking an Uber to the venue, but before I do, let me call my mom and tell her I'm leaving.

"Hello Mommy, I am on my way to the baby shower."

"Nante Yie Esi, we'll see you soon."

"All right Mommy, I will be safe."

During my ride to the venue, Amadi and I are texting. It has officially been a week into us talking, and I adore him so much. However, I got to keep my guard up so I don't get disappointed. Men will have you liking them in the beginning only to let you down. He already knows I'm off to the baby shower. He is attending a networking event hosted his friend in Jersey. I arrive at the shower amazed at the scenery. Everything was pink, blue and gold. At the center of the space was a balloon arch that read, "Boy? Or Girl?" There is a nice white couch and center table as well.

"Hey Esi, how are you?"

I recognize that voice from somewhere; it's my cousin Ewurama. I haven't seen her in ages. I look around to spot her. She's sitting down at a table with her husband. I go over to greet her. As soon as I walk over, tons of my family come to welcome me.

Aunt Susie was the chillest aunty I know, but that doesn't mean she isn't inquisitive. She's wearing her white kente outfit with lace detailing. It's so beautiful. She even has a head piece to match the ensemble. She addresses me first.

"Ete sen Esi."

"Auntie me ho yɛ medaase."

"I haven't seen you in a long time. How's you and that boy I seen you with?"

"Oh, Aunty, we are no longer together."

"Awurade Nyame! Jesus! What happened?"

"Nothing really, we just realized we weren't compatible for each other."

"Oh, oh Sorry."

"It happened months ago. I am completely over him."

"Ah Ha, I knew something was off when you came here alone. Anyways, my dear, gye gye w'ani. Enjoy yourself. Do not let the worries of life stress you. Your man of God is coming."

I don't know what to say. I nod. "Aunty, thank you."

"Esi, Mommy and Daddy are calling you. When did you come? You missed Samson and Anastasia's entrance." Ivy says. Ivy looks statuesque in her outfit that compliments her shape, and she rocks a curly pixie cut. Ivy is my oldest sibling and is the one that assumes the motherly role. As if I need more of that in my life. Everyone always treats me as a baby, being the youngest.

"I came a few minutes ago. I'm coming."

It doesn't occur to me that I'm late. I guess I overestimated the time it would start. Anastasia is wearing a gold lace dress with a long train. Samson wears a white suit with gold accents that compliments my sister's dress. She flashes me a smile. I walk over and embrace my immediate family, starting with my parents. In the Ghanaian culture, you must greet your elders as a sign of respect. My mom starts the event with a prayer.

"God, we thank you for bringing us together to celebrate Anastasia and Samson having their first child. Father, you have done so much in our lives, which we will forever be grateful. Bless the people in attendance. Make breakthroughs happen in their lives. You know what they need right now. Whatever they have been wanting, bestow it upon them at the right time. Bless Anastasia's unborn baby, may they be healthy and grow to full term. In Jesus' name we pray. May the grace of our Lord Jesus Christ, the love of God, and the fellowship of the Holy Spirit, be with us now and forevermore. Can everyone say Amen?"

Everyone says a resounding amen. My mom continues on to say, "Today is only the doing of the Lord. So, everyone should be happy. The food is ready, so make a line towards the back of the hall."

An assortment of Ghanaian party dishes are there. We have the usual jollof, fried rice, waakye, assorted meats, stew, meat pie, bofrot, etc. We even have a cake that is decorated exquisitely. It's a white and gold five-tier cake with flowers which had a monogram saying *Baby Danso* in gold. The food is so good and there's enough to feed the guests. My mom was the event planner. She makes everything come to life. She does this on the side for people as a source of income. The only people she'll do it for free is her children. My mom is the mastermind behind all the games we play. We have to figure out the circumference of her belly using ribbon. Next, we play "Drink the Baby Bottle," which is filled with juice. The fastest person wins. Then we do an egg toss. We have to make sure the egg is secure enough with tools on our table that when it falls, it will be unscathed. We also play Simon Says. I thoroughly enjoy myself.

Finally, we have to cast our ballot on the gender of the baby. I want it to be a girl, but my spirit is telling me it'll be a boy. I write *boy* and slip it in the box. Either way, I am going to love the baby just the same.

There is a professional photographer to take our family pictures. I haven't seen my entire family in a long time. So many people keep coming up to me. It's overwhelming, but I don't mind after a while. The star of the event, Anastasia, is taking pictures with everyone alongside her husband. Now, it's the time we have been waiting for. Anastasia and Samson grab champagne flutes and turn them upside down into the cake. When they pull the glasses up, it reveals blue frosting. Everyone screams for joy. Anastasia looks at her husband in amazement. He holds her in his arms and kisses her forehead. I go over to congratulate her. She really appreciates it. Remembering the fact that my sister has always wanted to be a wife and a mom in that order brings joy to my eyes. My whole family being in this space together for a celebration of life instead of grief is a blessing. The couple together open up the gifts that were given, thanking everyone in the process. They get tons of gifts for the baby. When it comes to my gift, Anastasia's smile turns big. She keeps thanking me for considering her in the gift. She mouths to me, "I love you." The center is open for dancing. The first person to dance is none other than my father. Soon after, people come to dance. It was a vibe.

The venue owners had a limit on the time we could be there until. We have to leave before 11pm. I help serve the cake and clean up. It's difficult to get the guest to leave, but we did. I carpool with my cousin Ewurama. She offers for her husband to drive me, and I'm grateful to her. I fall asleep immediately after changing into my comfy clothes. The next morning, I realize that I never texted Amadi back. I decided to do that later after my sermon.

The pastor preaching said, "Congratulations, the thing you have been waiting for will be yours. You will no longer weep over what you do not have." I just smile because I have reassurance that God will show out for me. He will place the right people in my path and align things for my good. Just as I'm going to text Amadi, he calls me.

Amadi and I have been enjoying each other's company, and I appreciate how it's been getting to know him thus far. He's a great man with intentionality and concern for others.

"Hey, I know you were out yesterday, so I didn't want to bother you. Just wanted to see how you're doing."

"I'm fine. I was about to reach out before you called. I fell asleep last night."

"How was the shower?"

"It was fun. So many of my family came. Guess what? My sister is having a boy!"

"Nice being with family it's important. What!? That's amazing news. Congrats to her."

"Yes, I'm going to be an aunt again. How was the networking event?"

"It was all right, but I'd rather hang out with you."

I pause for a second, which felt like forever. I mean, I'm starting to like him, but he can't know that. We are supposed to be friends.

"I bet you would've enjoyed yourself at the shower."

"Can I ask you a question?"

"Yes, you can."

"What would be your ideal day if you had no distractions?"

"I would love to get my nails and hair done. Then eat at a nice restaurant."

"What's stopping you from doing that?"

"I was going to do that, so nothing is stopping me. Except the nice restaurant thing. I never take myself out."

"What would you say if you did all these things? My treat."

"Really? You'd do that for me? Why? Is there a catch?"

"I think you are a good person and deserve to be pampered."

"Words can't explain how thankful I am to you."

"Don't mention it."

Once the phone call ends, I begin crying tears of joy. Thinking, *wow this man really is considerate.* As much as I love the kind gesture, I am more concerned with if he's doing this to use me. I can't help but feel this way. The men I have encountered have all disappointed me. Who's to say Amadi won't do the same? Maybe I am tripping and it's all in my head. Should I do it for the plot? Continue talking to him?

"See what will happen," I whisper. Only time will tell if he's genuine or hiding behind a façade. We all know men love to ginger you up in the beginning. Selling you a dream only to change with time. I'm not saying Amadi will do this, but you can never be too certain.

Anyways, let me check to see if I packed everything for my trip to Ghana. Just as I thought, I forgot to bring my lilac FujiFilm camera to take pictures. I want to make the best out of this experience, being that I haven't been to the motherland since I was a teen. I have my important documents needed to travel, such as my visa, passport, and yellow fever vaccination card. Zuhrah assures me that all the bridesmaids are attending the trip. This is going to be a relaxing vacation, and guess what? No work to worry about. I would love to travel for long periods of time. In an ideal world, I'd be rich enough to do that. We are manifesting that life one day. I look around my room and it's in a state of chaos. I put on my music and get to cleaning. African Gospel always puts me in the mood. I come to the realization that I have so many clothes I either can't fit or don't mesh well with my current style.

My phone rings and it's Anastasia. I rarely get calls from her, so this will be interesting.

"Hey Esi, I wanted to call to thank you for coming to my baby shower. Your presence meant a lot to me."

"Aww thanks, Anastasia. I am so happy that you're having a boy, and I wouldn't miss seeing you during this beautiful moment of your life."

"No problem. I know I don't say this a lot, but I love you and want our relationship to be better. If you need anyone to talk to, I'm always a call away. How's planning for your trip going?"

I'm not sure if it's the pregnancy hormones that are kicking in, but she's been nicer. She is changing for the better.

"Thank you, sis, I feel the same way. I know our relationship has been rocky, but just know I'm here for you as well. My trip planning is going well. I finished packing my luggage, but not my carry-on. Still debating if I should bring one."

"I know, but we are sisters, and just know you have a friend in me. Don't bring too many things. You don't want your bag to be overweight, because you'll have to pay more."

"Thank you, and I forgot about that. I should bring an empty carry-on to bring back souvenirs."

After a while, we talk about her giving birth. She is nervous about the pain but excited to see her baby. My only concern is the hospital she will go to. I hope she gets the proper care, because black women have a high mortality rate during pregnancy. It's tough getting proper care when professionals don't take your concerns seriously because you are seen as strong and having a high pain tolerance. I do not want my sister to suffer the same fate, which is what I pray against. My wish is for her to recover and be healthy for her child. I don't want her to have postpartum issues. We eventually get off the phone. I feel better about our relationship with each other. It speaks on the growth of us as siblings. We have certainly come a long way and I'm forever grateful for it.

A few days after, on a Wednesday, Amadi keeps to his word on treating me to a day of relaxation. This man really shows me that I'm capable of being cared for. My presence means so much to him that he's willing to make me happy without expecting anything. That is a genuine person. I got my nails and hair done. My nails are 3-D flowers on two fingers and the rest are pink. My hair is done in small knotless braids with some light brown highlights. Normally I don't get color with braids too often, but I figure why not try something new. The color looks great against my mahogany skin tone. I have my solo dinner date, which is peaceful; in fact, it did not feel awkward at all. I enjoy my own company. Days feel long leading up to the trip, which I found odd. May this trip be good to me. God, show me how good it will get.

GHANA, MY MOTHERLAND!!

TODAY IS THE DAY I HAVE BEEN AWAITING. MONTHS OF PLANNING have finally come to this very moment. Zuhrah creates a group chat with all the bridesmaids. She asks if we are heading to JFK airport right now. I text along with most of the girls that we're on our way. Before leaving, I pray for safe travels and protections on the airplane. The ride to the airport brings immense tranquility to me. I know that it will be a great trip filled with adventure. I make sure to leave my house early to beat the traffic and start the long process at the TSA line. Finally, I am by the Delta Airlines section of JFK Airport. I spot Zuhrah waiting. Once she sees me, her face lights up and she begins smiling. We give each other a warm embrace. We haven't seen much of one another since the Atlantic City trip.

"What is taking everyone so long? I have been waiting for everybody to arrive, and you are the first one on time."

"I'm sorry for making you wait, I thought I was early."

"No, I'm sorry for freaking out. I just like to be early for things so we don't miss our flight or have to rush to our terminal."

No less than ten minutes after Zuhrah had her mini meltdown did all the bridesmaids come strolling in except for one. She's no longer upset but relieved that they are mostly here.

"I'm glad you are all here," Zuhrah says.

They are all excited to be going on the trip and embrace each other. So, here's the rundown on the bridesmaids. Aiysha is a tall and slender brown-skinned woman who looks like she does model. I find out she does in fact model for runways and has been doing so for five years now. She is married with two girls. She likes the hectic lifestyle.

Makena walks in with a blonde blunt cut bob. She has on Chanel glasses with a bag to match. She is an optometrist doing her residency, which she has worked hard to achieve. Daisy has a 90s pixie cut that compliments her so well. She is a software developer and loves what she does. Gisella had on brown boho twists which flatter her brown skin. She is a high school teacher and enjoys making an impact on teens. Willow is the last to walk in. She has lemonade braids giving diva vibes as soon as she walks in. She recently got married to the love of her life and is a career counselor. She helps others explore different career options. All of us are successful with our own careers. This brings me immense joy to see black women excel.

Zuhrah says, "I'm so glad that all of you have arrived. This is going to be a good trip. I am beyond grateful to you all for being here with me. Love you all."

We all say in unison that we love Zuhrah, which makes her smile and say, "Aww, you girls." We start to check our bags in at the airport and get our tickets. After we pay for our bags, it's time to go into the TSA line. As usual, it's a long wait. Once we each show our passports, it's time to get our carry-ons scanned and go through the detectors. It doesn't take long. Gisella has the idea for us to get some snacks and drinks before we board the plane. Since we haven't eaten anything yet. Everyone gets the food they want. We decide it's time to walk to our terminal and wait for our flight.

While we're waiting, we get to know each other better. One at a time, we all say our names and a little fact about ourselves. I remember Daisy because she has a fun spirit about her. She loves to bake pastries and is thinking about owning a storefront. A total of an hour passes before we are allowed to board the plane. I notice that we are all scattered into different seats in the airplane. I have the window seat and next to me are Zuhrah and Daisy. Throughout the plane ride, I have on my headphones and am watching movies and listening to music. The plane ride is a total of ten hours and thirty minutes. Zuhrah and Daisy fall asleep, only waking up when it's time for us to eat and arrive at Kotoka International Airport. Before we land, so many people on board are clapping and saying, "Thank you, Lord."

People are in a rush to leave the plane, making it difficult to leave quickly and efficiently. After twenty to thirty minutes of waiting, we officially get off the plane. I'm tired and the more we wait for our luggage to arrive from the carousel, the more exhausted I feel. Thankfully, we all get our suitcases and are able to leave. Abronoma is our personal driver who is waiting for us the minute we leave the airport. He has a huge van for us, similar to a trotro but upscale and modern. Zuhrah is the one who got us the driver, which I will forever be grateful to her for doing. Abronoma is truly kind to all of us, helping to pack our bags into the van. I am the first to notice when we arrive at our Airbnb house in Accra.

As we enter the house, so many thoughts come to mind. I am astonished by the beauty seen all around. We are in a three-story house and each one of us had our own room. It is a three and a half bath. Looking at the architecture of the place, I can tell there was attention to detail. From the African-inspired artwork seen throughout the house to the décor in the home. Willow had a hand in us choosing this place with her keen eyes. We all settle into our rooms. I choose the one on the third floor so that I can be out the way and in my own world.

I must take a shower I say to myself. I have all my personal care items laid out and my clothes. No less than five minutes after I connect into the WiFi do I get tons of notifications popping up. My eyes light up when I see one from Amadi. He sent me a message on WhatsApp.

AMADI:

Hey Esi, I know you may not see this until later, but I wanted to wish you a safe flight and may God protect you during your time in Ghana. When you get this, please give me a text. Hope you enjoy your time. I can't wait to see you after your trip. I will be missing you a lot.

As soon as I see this message, I immediately call him on video chat. I wasn't sure if he'd still be up because of the time zone difference, being that Ghana is 4 hours ahead. He picked up, smiling at me.

"Hey Esi, I hope you are well."

"Hi, I am feeling a bit of jet-lag but other than that, I'm happy I arrived safely by God's grace."

"Yes, we thank God. I just want to say I'm missing you and wish we could go out for a date. I can't wait for us to see one another after your trip."

Did this man just say he missed me? That's a big step, because I didn't think we'd be at this stage yet. I mean, I'm not his girlfriend. I keep this thought to myself and play along.

"Yeah, I know, but you'll see me soon. We can still talk from time to time if you would like."

"Yes, I would love that. So, you aren't going out tonight?"

"As of now, I don't think so. I'm not even hungry just really tired. Sleep is calling my name."

Just as we are talking, I get a knock on my door. It's Makena standing at the door. I tell Amadi to hold on for a moment while I talk to her.

"Hey Esi, the girls and I want to order some food. Would you be down? I know you are starving as well."

"Sure, now that you mention it, my hunger is coming back. Can you order me waakye with stew and goat meat and a malt drink?"

"Wow girl, you know what you want already. I will make sure to get as you wish."

"Haha. Thank you so much. I will Zelle you the money, just let me know my part."

"I will. I'll leave you to relax." During this whole interaction, I forget that Amadi is still on the phone. I thought he'd hang up and call me later. As the patient person he is, he stayed on the phone.

"Hey Amadi, I'm back."

"Hey, my love, I thought you weren't hungry."

"I thought so too, but I started to get hungry talking to Makena. I'm just a girl, you know."

"I understand a girl that needs food. Anyways, how long are you going to be away on vacation?"

"I am staying for two weeks," I say with a smile.

"Wow, look at you, minister of enjoyment. I hope you have the most fun you can out there. I'm jealous, we are only in PR for the week."

"I will, and you have fun in Puerto Rico. I know it will be an amazing time. Make sure our groom is on his best behavior."

He looks at me with a serious expression in his eyes and says, "I give you my word I will make sure he's safe. Don't worry, he only has good intentions for Zuhrah. So, no wandering eyes on his end."

I want to trust him, but men can lie, so I am very weary with listening.

"You better keep to it."

"I can never let you down, Esi."

All this talking has me thinking about his plans with us in the future. "Anyways, I have a question for you, sir?"

"Ask anything your heart desires."

"Okay, so what are your intentions with me, exactly?"

"I have feelings for you that run deep, Esi. Since the first time I saw you. My intentions are to build a future with you."

Ehh Awurade, I did not know he was serious. If this is from you, Lord let your will be done. Raising my brows at him, I ask, "You sure that's what you want?"

"I'm certain. People like you only come once in a lifetime. I would be silly to let you go."

Is it hot in here or is it just me? Am I starting to feel nervous suddenly?

There is no way this man has strong feelings for me. I can't help but feel the same way about him now, but I can't let him know that yet.

"Thank you for saying that. It means a lot to me."

"No problem. Now that the cat's out of the bag, how about we continue dating?"

"We most certainly can." *He's being very intentional, is this even real?*

I get a knock on my door. It's Makena with food in her hand. "Thank you so much. How much do I owe you?"

"You owe me 211 ccdis which is roughly twenty dollars. You can send it to me whenever. Have a good night. We have an impactful morning ahead of us. Don't forget to wake up early for our historical sightseeing."

I nod my head and say, "Thank you."

By then Amadi and I have been talking for an hour. "Hey Amadi, I'm going to shower, then eat. I will speak with you tomorrow. Feel free to talk to me when you can."

"Okay, will do. Enjoy your meal and have a great night's rest."

"Thank you, good night." After our call, I take a much-needed shower and eat my food. In that moment, I also send Makena money via a money transfer app. The waakye was so appetizing. It consists of rice and black-eyed peas, shito, stew, boiled egg and spaghetti. This meal alone put me to sleep.

The next morning, I wake up feeling like I should get more sleep, but the girls want to go to both the Cape Coast and Elmina Slave Castles today if time allows. I get myself ready and go downstairs. Some of the girls are waiting in the living room, including Makena and Gisella. They both greet me as I walk down the stairs.

"Hey girls, how's it going?"

In unison, they both say, "Good." Makena speaks after.

"Did you like your food last night?"

"That food satisfied my appetite."

"I'm glad it did." During our conversation the rest of the bridesmaids, Willow and Daisy, including Zuhrah, come waltzing down the stairs.

Zuhrah brings the energy, saying, "Good morning my loves, are we ready for the day ahead of us? It's going to be touching and life changing."

We all say yes and nod our heads. We wait a total of ten minutes before Abronoma comes with his van, ready to take us to Cape Coast Castle. While in the car, all these thoughts flash through my mind. I am so grateful to be here. People went through suffering for us to have freedom.

The ride took us approximately three hours and thirty-seven minutes since we are coming from Accra, the capital. The scenery of the castle is beautiful with the view of the Atlantic Ocean. We decide to go with a tour guide. The tour is eye opening and moving. All this is heartbreaking when you think about the transatlantic slave trade, which transported millions of slaves across the Atlantic Ocean to the Americas. As we walked through the dungeon, a sense of desolation filled my heart. We were told that up to 1,500 slaves were kept in a dungeon awaiting the next ship. There were not any bathrooms, so people would urinate and defecate on themselves. *How inhumane? One can only imagine the terror they witnessed at the hands of colonizers.*

"Hey girly, are you feeling all right?" Makena asks me.

"Yeah, but this is a lot to take in. Slavery shaped a lot of things we see today."

"I know, take it easy. This is a learning experience."

I have to take a breather first before continuing with the tour.

I learned that Ghana was referred to as Gold Coast prior to gaining independence in 1957. The castle was built in the 1650s. People were taken from neighboring countries, and some died on their journey to Ghana. There is a door of return which symbolizes the resilient nature of African descendants who visit their homeland. In contrast, there is the door of no return, which was the point of contact for slaves that was taken to the Americas. This experience taught me to be grateful for the opportunities life has afforded me. The castle has quotes from famous leaders and freedom fighters such as the likes of Kwame Nkrumah, Ghana's first president.

The next stop is Elmina Castle. The place was roughly twenty minutes away from the Cape Coast castle. Walking through this place is easier than the previous location. Probably because I calmed myself with mindful breathing. A few facts about the fortress are that it was built by the Portuguese in 1482 and was originally for trading goods such as gold and ivory. Some years down the line, the British acquired it for 85 years and was the first trading post for slaves in all of sub-Saharan Africa. It is known as one of the world heritage sites. In 1997, Elmina became a museum. Looking at the water gives a chilling reminder of the slaves that were thrown in the ocean. I pray that God blesses the people and their lineage who suffered such hardships. With that being said, this lights a flame within me to better myself. I am deserving of the best out of life.

Everyone is craving food. We decide to eat at the Anomansa restaurant, which is in Elmina. We get Attieke with fried fish, Light soup with chicken and rice, fried rice with chicken, jollof with goat meat and assorted rice which includes jollof/fried rice with veggies, spices and sausage with chicken and beef. One could say we have a feast. Zuhrah starts the conversation while we are eating.

"How did everyone find the experience being here?"

Gisella says, "It was emotional but empowering."

I add, "A lot of the atrocities of this world is because people thought they were superior to others based on their own ideologies and imposed so much harm."

The girls all nod in agreement with me.

Zuhrah is like, "Wow, I think you said what we all were thinking. I felt chills just hearing the history."

To see the places where the slave trade happened is very emotional and brings me to tears. May their souls rest in peace.

We have a much-needed conversation about racism, and I'm glad we did.

One thing I adore about Ghana is how welcoming the people are. They're polite to everyone. Showing respect and having manners is an integral part of the culture. Foreigners feel like they belong. You see Black people from the diaspora being given traditional Ghanaian names and received with open arms. It brings me much joy to be from here.

After that, we head on the road back to Accra. Along the way, we also decided to get e-sims for phone service during our stay. Once I have service, I'm flooded with messages from my parents. I text the family group chat and say I arrived in Ghana safely. They are pleased that I reached out to them, but wished I had done so sooner. I am an old lady, so as soon as I have the ability, I take a nap. I wake up an hour later feeling all right. Realizing I have been in my room too long, I make my way downstairs to speak with the girls. Aiysha is there and suggests we go out to see the nightlife.

"I have been searching places to go in Accra, and I think we'd enjoy Bloom Bar Restaurant. What do you think, Esi?" she adds.

"I think it's a good idea. I'm down as long as it's okay with the rest of the girls."

Eventually the bridal squad comes down and is on board for some fun. I run upstairs to get ready. My hair is in small knotless braids. So, styling it will be easy. We each get ready in our y2k baddie outfits. The outfits are cute. I have on a pink beret hat, white airbrush styled top that says "Established 90s Baby," with a pleated pink skirt, nice kitten heels, gold bamboo hoops that have my name plated in pink font, and rimless sunglasses. The makeup is immaculate. I do a white smoky eye. I take some selfies using a digital camera. I notice the pictures come out so much better on a camera than a phone. I must say, *I look good.* I knock on Zuhrah's door.

"Esi, my love, you look fabulous."

"Thank you, sweetie. So do you! I love the baggy jeans."

"Aww, you think so? I was second-guessing this look."

"Yes, sis, you look stunning." It takes us an hour to finish getting ready.

Abronoma was kind enough to drop us off at the restaurant. The atmosphere is great walking into, and the music is on point. They play afrobeats music the entire night which has me on Cloud Nine. The drinks we have are virgin daiquiri mango and passion fruit. All of us have two drinks. We are advised to be aware of our surroundings because people can tell you are a foreigner. Once they pick up on that, you're an easy target. So, we stay together and remain vigilant the entire time. We don't leave the place until 5 am. I always heard that Ghana's party scene was worthwhile, but I didn't believe it until now. Sleep deprived is an understatement to how I feel going home.

"Hey girls, get your rest now because at 1 pm, we will be going to the Independence Square," Zuhrah says.

I'm filled with joy anticipating our photo shoot. Before we arrive at the house, we decide to get street food. *Hausa koko and bofrot it is*, I think to myself. Hausa koko is a spicy smooth porridge made with millet.

This is my first time having Hausa koko and it's amazing paired with the sweetness of bofrot. I sleep so well following this meal. By the time I wake up, it's 11 am and Amadi had texted me a thought-felt message.

AMADI:

> Hey Esi, just checking on you to see how you're faring in the motherland GH. I hope you enjoy yourself and have an experiential time there. Missing you and wishing I was there.

ESI:

> Hey Amadi, thank you for checking on me. I have been loving my time here. How is PR? Did I read that right? You miss me?

AMADI:

> I'm glad to know that. Puerto Rico is amazing. We did ATV riding and had so much fun. Although it was quite the adventure. You read that right. I miss you, being here isn't the same without you.

ESI:

> Wow, you like the thrill of ATV riding. I could never do that. I'm too much of a scaredy cat. I'm glad you enjoyed yourself. That touches my heart to know you miss me.

AMADI:

> I love basking in the outdoors. What can I say, I'm a risk taker. If I'm lying, I'm flying. I mean every word. What are you doing today?

ESI:

I can tell. How sincere. The girls and I are going to Independence Square to have a photoshoot at the arch. I am so excited.

AMADI:

Thanks, I hope you have fun. Can't wait to see your photos.

ESI:

No problem. I am about to get ready, I'll talk to you when I can.

AMADI:

Okay, talk to you later. My supermodel.

ESI:

I can't with you. Bye

I completely lost track of time. Let me get ready. Zuhrah has us all wearing the same style satin dress. It's a cowl neck pleated split A-line dress. All the bridesmaids, including me, are wearing dusty rose dresses while our bride wears a hot pink version. *Ooo, we about to look so alluring in these dresses. I'm here for it.* I do a natural glam beat on my face. Then I head downstairs to see if the girls are ready. To my surprise, we all are coming down at the same time.

"We ready?" Zuhrah says.

We say a resounding yes and yell, "We Outside!"

Arriving at the Independence Square brings a smile to my face. Our photographer is waiting for us with his gear in hand.

"Ladies, I am Dodzi from VisionCreativeGH, nice to meet you all. I will take individual pictures, followed by a group picture."

We each take our own photos waving the Ghana flag. I ask Dodzi to look at my images and when I say he captured me beautifully, I mean it. Then we take a group picture with Zuhrah in the middle. The dresses are flowing and bodies glistening in the sun. I'm amazed by the number of stares we got from passersby. We're listening to "Bring Back the Love" by Akwaboah. The vibes are there. Dodzi is talented in his craft. We go back to the house and change into more comfortable clothing so we can grab something to eat nearby.

Daisy calls out to us, saying, "Hey I saw this restaurant called Buka. I think it will be fun. We should go."

"I'm down. What do the rest of y'all think?" The girls agree with Daisy and I.

Getting ready is a chore. I can't decide between two outfits. I go with a yellow dress with a mock neck and pleats at the bottom. It suits my body very well.

All I do is touch up my makeup and style my hair.

"Knock-Knock, it is me, Zuhrah. Are you ready, Esi?"

"Actually, just finished. I'm coming down now."

"All right, girl, you look so beautiful. Love the dress, it accentuates your skin tone."

"Thank you, my love."

As soon as I meet up with the girls, we are out the door. *Buka Restaurant, here we come!* The ambiance is so nice over here. I hope the food is worth the travel. The environment has an eccentric feeling to it. There is African wall art. After we are seated, we wait for our food and drinks. The presentation is nice. I get angwamo, which is a meal that has oil rice, fried eggs, sardines, shito, and sausages. I ask for toolo beef on the side, and my beverage of choice is a fresh mango juice.

"How's your food, ladies?" the waiter asks.

"Everything is fantastic." The girls agree.

"Can I get dessert? I want dulce de leche ice cream," I say.

"Okay, I'll be right back."

Moments later, the waiter comes with my ice cream. It's reminiscent of the Haagen Daz's flavor. After the meal I just had, my stomach feels satisfied. We pay and go back to the house. Zuhrah suggests we have a bonding activity.

"I have a card game we can play, called Girls Room Game. I think we should play tonight at like 9 pm. It will be fun."

This is going to be interesting. I go upstairs and take off my makeup, take a shower, and dress in comfy clothes. As usual, I take a nap, which makes me feel energized. I hear music coming from downstairs. This leads me to check the time and it's 8:30 pm. Being my inquisitive self, I leave my room to see what surprise lies ahead. The sitting area has been decorated in pink and gold. "Welcome to Game Night, Esi." Gisella says.

"Thank you!"

"Come grab a bite and sit down, the game will start."

Entering the area, I scope the scenery and notice a charcuterie board with some savory and sweet options. Along with beverages. *Oh, wow, when did they do this? They really outdid themselves. Let me grab a snack.* I sit down in one of the available seats. Zuhrah begins speaking.

"Hey, my friends. Thank you for being on this trip with me. To show you I care, I got each of you something I thought you'd like."

The gift is a surprise to me. Unwrapping the box, I see a bracelet with my name engraved on it with African beading and an adinkra symbol charm. The symbol I got was Nyame Nti, which means 'by God's grace,' and symbolizes faith and trust in God. I look over and each of us has a different charm with a different meaning. *She was intentional about the gift.*

"Thank you, Zuhrah, it is beautiful. I appreciate you so much."

"You're welcome, my love. It's game time!"

She pulls out a box with a deck of cards that says 'Girls Room Game.'

"The rules of the game are as follows. Each of us will pick a card and read off it. We all take turns answering the question without judgement. Let's begin."

Zuhrah starts first. "What is your ideal partner? Well, well this is an easy question. I would say I'm marrying my ideal partner. He is God-fearing, chivalrous, respectful, and intelligent."

The rest of us add on to what was already spoken. *My partner must love me like a true 90s man, otherwise, what's the point? I refuse to hold the sentiment that good men don't exist.* The second person is Gisella, and she get the question, "What are your dating dealbreakers?"

"I can't stand a man that's not considerate of other people's feelings, one that lies, does drugs, and abuses alcohol."

We all clap our hands in agreement. *Anyone that abuses substances to cope with reality needs to get professional help.*

Willow's question is about dating horror stories.

"I have been shown shege. What difficult situation have I not experienced because of a man. I got cheated on by one of my exes. He said, and I quote it, 'Why are you so boring? I cheat because I am unhappy with the way things are going.' He wanted me to be someone I'm not. It all changed when I met my now-husband. He supports and loves me for the person I am."

Each of us have our own stories because wonders shall never end with dating. *After my experiences with Seth and Kobby, cautious is my state of mind.* Aiysha's question is juicy.

"Have you ever been attracted to your friend? I was interested in one of my guy friends and he didn't feel the same way. We tried being friends, but we fell out shortly after. Oh well, I guess." She shrugs her shoulders.

I never had a crush on my guy friends because I respect our friendship too much to date them. Plus, it becomes hella awkward when feelings are involved.

Makena is after Aiysha. She gets the question asking who her crush is. "This question is a no brainer, it's my husband, of course. What kind of silly question is that?"

I am afraid to admit this, but Amadi is growing on me and I kinda like it. Who knew I'd be over the men that hurt me before.

Daisy is the second to last one. Her question asks what her love language is. "Don't get me started on love languages. They are an amazing way of communicating how you like to be loved. If I had to choose, it would be quality time, receiving gifts, and physical touch. I picked these because I love spending time with my partner even if it means doing nothing. Second, who doesn't like getting gifts that are deliberately thought out, and I love to hug my partner and hold hands."

I on the other hand, love words of affirmation, quality time, and acts of service. When someone does something nice for me or says encouraging words, that brings me joy.

Finally, it's me. *Last but not least.* "What is your ideal wedding? Oh, this is a good one. My dream wedding would have to be a Ghanaian traditional and white wedding. I want a medium to big sized wedding with several outfit changes," I say in a laughing tone. "I want flowers everywhere and 90s themed décor. Oh, and my man better cry when I walk down the aisle."

My question gets the ball rolling with further think pieces about color scheme, locations, and venues. We talk about destination weddings, which are beautiful but extremely expensive depending on the country. We are having a great evening. *Zuhrah is such a thoughtful and kind friend.*

"Girls I have an announcement. We are going to a pottery class. So, bring your creative skills with you," Zuhrah announces. We are singing to the plethora of songs being played until we get tired and go to sleep.

The next morning, I feel like I overslept, but in fact, I woke up early for my standards. I get ready for the day in lounge clothes and shoes because I know I'll be getting messy with the clay. I even pull my hair in a half-up, half-down hairstyle. I decide to put on my Dior perfume as my scent of the day. On the way to the pottery class, I receive a meme about missing someone from Amadi that makes me chuckle. As a result, we exchange memes with one another. You can say we get each other's sense of humor. *He thinks he cute.* This thought makes me roll my eyes. When we arrive, we are greeted by our instructor and shown what to do. There is a model sculpture to follow. It's a bowl. At the pottery class, I really gain some skills. Although mine looks nothing like the model, it's still nice. I love the experience, it's relaxing. We get some food to go at the roadside, which was check check, a meal with fried rice with chicken and Ghana styled salad on the side. FanIce ice cream was our sweet treat of choice.

The food satisfies my hunger. This is a chill day, to be honest. Nothing much happened, which was nice for a change. I spend the rest of the day talking to the girls and building connections with some of them. Makena, Daisy, and Aiysha are funny and insightful about their careers. The next day, I go with Zuhrah to her dress fitting, which is early in the morning. It's for her traditional wedding. She doesn't want to fully commit to her kente dress without trying it out first. I'm impressed by her look. She is stunning. Her kente was made in Bonwire and has adinkra symbols such as gye nyame, sankofa which means 'learn from the past,' nyame dua which symbolizes Gods' presence and protection, duafe which means 'beauty,' akoma, which is the heart, and nyame nti. She was very mindful about using symbols that she cherishes. To her it's Ghanaian culture being represented.

We also figure out the bedazzled fans that we will wear for the wedding as well. The bridesmaids plan to go to Makola Market to buy a few things. While we are there, it's busy, but the atmosphere is lively. We get waist beads, handbags, head wraps, and jewelry. Everyone is very polite and kind. After that, we are off to the Labadi Beach. The environment is spectacular, and the water is clear. While walking, I marvel at the beauty of the beachfront. We are approached by people asking if we want to do horseback riding. *Why not? It couldn't hurt.* Getting on the horse is scary, but I do it anyway. The ride is fun, and I feel exhilarated trying something I never did before on the beach. We take videos of our ride for memories. Daisy spots a restaurant called Akwaaba, which is inside a hotel. I get something different for a change. A grilled beef burger with bacon and onion rings on the side. The food is delicious.

As we return to the house, I feel so grateful. Who am I to be in Ghana surrounded by wonderful people? I am enjoying myself. The life I built for myself is coming to fruition. I finally met a guy that likes me more than I know. *God, I'm so blessed. Thank you.* In the same breath, I just want to make sure Amadi isn't taking me for an idiot. Men can put up a façade to make you believe them. Most people are cool, but they are not solid. Discernment is important so you don't get your feelings hurt. Especially when someone doesn't live up to your perception of them that they created. Anyways, God always reveals things at the right time. People's character and true intentions come to the surface if they're faking it. Happiness that radiates from within is what I'm creating for myself.

Zuhrah and Gisella have the idea of us having a karaoke night. One thing about Zuhrah: she finds something to do. She produces great ideas and is a visionary. She is very caring about other's feelings. Her fiancé is lucky to have her, and he better know it. It's one of the many qualities I love about my bestie. Singing to our heart's content was fun. Everyone let loose and didn't have a care in the world. We played Beyoncé, Kesha Cole, 90s pop, R&B music, and much more. One song we sang that was a hit was by The Supremes titled "You Can't Hurry

Love." I have been wanting to collect vinyl records of artists for a long time. Maybe I should start that up when I get home. It reminds me of the show *Sister Sister*, when Tia and Tamera sing that song. I am not much of a singer, but that doesn't matter to me. I have that burst of energy. Once I get out of my shell, it's over. I begin showing my true silly self. *What can I say? I'm the life of the party.* I love my own company and so do others.

Two days later, after celebrating and doing an obstacle course we go to church. As I'm at church, the feelings come flooding through, causing me to have a tingling sensation. I can't control it. Lately I have been feeling so grateful for how my life is going. To think a few months after getting my heart broken, not only did I find a new sense of happiness, but purpose. *God, you are so wonderful.* I observe the fashion displayed and it's a remarkable sight. The variety of styles and colors are amazing. Like they say, God and fashion go together. One thing that stood out was 1 Corinthians 13:1-3. It talks about having unconditional love for others. This thought came to mind. *I can be successful, but without treating people with love and giving them grace, I'm nothing.* It costs nothing to be kind and show others you care.

The way I'm shaking and waving my handkerchief needs to be studied. I think it's a Ghanaian thing to dance with a handkerchief. Not only do I see that, but some women have tambourines. It's really a skillful art to know how to play these types of instruments effortlessly. Then you have the drummers and guitarist, which is music to my ears. I feel the spirit of the Lord around and I can tell the bridal party does as well. My walk with God hasn't always been perfect. It has been met with challenges, but through it all, my parent's teachings remind me to keep going. We go to get food from a nice upscale restaurant, then call it a day.

The fact that this is our last week in Ghana is making me so filled with grief. I will make the best of my time here. Anyways, guess where we're off to? The Kwame Nkrumah memorial park. It is very nice to pay homage to Ghana's first president. The mausoleum is the burial site of Dr. Kwame Nkrumah and his wife Fathia Nkrumah. We see the bronze statue which is the same place that Ghana got its independence in 1957. The museum highlights the president's life history and images of him alongside famous figures. We walk through this beautiful garden that has trees planted by various leaders. Along with flowers and water fountains, there are sculptures of flute players.

Subsequently after sightseeing, we go to a Thai restaurant. The food is wonderful. I have a lot to eat including Thai spring rolls, fried rice with beef, fried chicken wings, and their signature drink Thailand blue. Everything is good about today. I get a random text from my mom that comes as a surprise.

MOM:

> Esi my darling, mesoo daeε bi faa wo ho. Is there something you are not telling me?

ESI:

> You had a dream about me? Can you tell me, what was it about?

MOM:

> Na wo ne aberante bi wɔ hɔ. Are you dating someone right now?

ESI:

> Are you sure you had a dream about me and a man, or did someone tell you?

MOM:

> You know I can't lie to you. That's what happened in the dream. So, I decided to come and ask you myself.

ESI:

> If you must know, yes, I am.

MOM:

> Ei, so why haven't you told me?

ESI:

> Mommy, I didn't tell you because I'm not his girlfriend yet.

MOM:

Well, my dear, it's only a matter of time. I pray for you all the time that God will allow you to marry a man that loves and adores you.

ESI:

Thank you, Mommy. From your lips to God's ears.

MOM:

Amen. I hope you enjoy the rest of your trip. God be with you.

ESI:

Thank you, I will. Talk to you later, Mommy.

MOM:

All right, I will see you when you come back.

I wonder how my mom had a dream about me dating before I could tell anyone else. African parents always say they had a dream about you. They are spiritually in tune. Life is about to get remarkably interesting for me. I can just feel everything aligning for my greatest good. In the midst of it all, God's grace sustained me. It is funny how things work out for you when you focus on the good in life. The next day, we go to the Kakum National Park. We get across the famous canopy walkway. It's nerve wracking and terrifying being high up, but we do it. I keep my prayers in mind the whole time. We also see various animals around such as monkeys, antelopes, and forest elephants.

As always, when we return, we have to get some food. We opt for some street food which includes chichinga with suya spice, kelewele, and chofi. We even have sobolo as our drink of choice. Once we arrive back to the house, we just sit down and have a conversation about our experiences.

"I had my misconceptions about Ghana. I thought it wasn't as welcoming as people make it seem. When we were growing up, I used to hear insensitive questions like, 'do you see lions and live in huts?'

They would make clicking noises as if that's how everyone in Africa communicates. It wasn't until I got older that I had a newfound appreciation for being African," Zuhrah says.

"Mmhmm, that's very true and now with the wave of afrobeats and *Black Panther*, suddenly everyone wants to be African," I say.

Everyone agrees with both of us. "It feels like being African is the new wave. While that's nice, people still do not accept us. People want to try our food but then disrespect it," Aiysha says.

We all have similar experiences and viewpoints on this matter. This was an interesting conversation about diaspora wars between Black people and African immigrants. This has been happening for years but with the rise of media highlighting African culture has benefited us. Coming to Ghana as an adult made me realize that the division that was created amongst us abroad seldom exists here. There's an emphasis on community. Although, there are issues with colorism rooted in years of slavery. Especially with the consistent need to use skin bleaching agents to appease others while damaging their skin. As well as some systemic problems. I notice there is togetherness and bliss. It's time we unite with one another. There's no need for division. When it comes down to it, we bleed the same. Teaching my future kids to love their melanin and Afrocentric features is crucial so they don't lose their cultural identity. I love how we can have deep conversations that matter the most.

Three days are remaining, and it's hitting us all that we will be back in New York City. Although I feel this way, I am going to live up my remaining time. Also, I have the bridal shower to prepare for and attend. I can't wait for Zuhrah to become Mrs. Bamidele. She deserves a love that supersedes the love she gives to others. However, today we go to a Batik Tye and Dye workshop. It's interesting making my own tie and dye patterned cloth. I have so much fun stamping the fabric with designs. The instructor is extremely helpful. They are experienced and knew their stuff. The good part is that we get to take the finished product with us. We decide to buy souvenirs and food to take with us back home to NYC. I'm able to get a gift for Amadi as a thank you for being a great person to me. It is a kente print top that I think might fit him. *Am I falling in love?* Overall, it's a good day of learning.

The second to last day is filled with emotions. When I tell you I'm dreading leaving. Enjoyment is sweet o. I am grateful for this experience and wish it didn't have to end. I will go back to Ghana again and see some family, although most of them live abroad now in places like America, England, and Germany. We go to an obstacle course, and it is so exhilarating to do. I thought I would not be able to do it, but I do. There is so much to do, each part is increasingly nerve-wracking. All the girls have similar experiences. Despite it all, we motivate each other to continue. That's what I appreciate the most about this girl's trip. We can bond over anything and there is no pettiness or arguments. We also decide to have a girl's night out for our official last day. It was a night club called 1102 Night Club, which is fun. I mean the music is blasting and we're looking cutesy. I feel good vibes being here. What a profound way to end our trip.

"Can't believe it's time to leave for New York," Aiysha says. Sadness clouds her features.

"Yeah, Aiysha this trip went by fast. I could spend a month or more here if I could."

"The motherland always gives that effect, but money has to be made, and life must go on. But we have memories, hahaha."

"Yes, that's absolutely true. We need money for everything it seems."

"That's what adulting has taught us all."

"Let us get ready to leave."

As I finish packing, my main excitement comes from being able to lay in bed and sleep after our plane ride. I guess I have gotten to the age where staying indoors brings me peace of mind. No less than thirty minutes later, it's time for us to leave. We say our prayers and then head out the door. Abronoma is waiting for us outside. We do a quick stop for some food that we eat on our way. We arrive at the airport on time and wave our driver goodbye.

The entire process of being in the airport and catching a flight is draining. We pay for our luggage and go through customs. I forget how long and tedious it can be, but nevertheless, we make it on the plane. The flight is long, but it feels like a breeze, thankfully. The food is not to my expectations, but it's still edible. All I do is sleep for the most part. We finally arrive at JFK Airport ten hours later. Getting off the plane isn't easy. As to be expected, people are in a rush to leave, but I mean, why? Especially when most of us must walk over to the baggage claim and wait for our luggage. I wish the area wasn't far from the terminal we're at. Finally, after walking for a few minutes and waiting for our suitcases, it's time to go our separate ways. Everyone embraces each other one last time. I walk towards the taxi/car service section, where I request my Uber and head home. What a journey it has been, and to God be the glory.

Chapter Six

L.O.V.E IS WHAT I WAS WAITING FOR

"So, are you going to tell me where we're going, Amadi?" It's officially been a week since I've been back and man, I miss being around him. *Is that weird?*

"I can't right now, it'll ruin the surprise. Just be patient."

"Okay, okay, if you say so, but before you do, I have a surprise for you."

"Really? All right, what is it?"

I hand him the Kente shirt.

"Oh, wow, an Ankara top. I love the patterns, it's nice."

He gives me a warm embrace. The smell of sweet cologne fills my nostrils. "It's a Kente material with traditional colors such as gold, yellow, green, red, and black. I am glad you love it. It's a token of my appreciation for being kind to me."

"I learn something new every day. You are deserving of all the good things life has to offer."

I grow silent. Not sure if it's nerves, but I have nothing left to say. Amadi planned a beautiful date night at Skywise, I wonder where we're off to next. My heart is beating fast which is odd. He drives us to this venue in Brooklyn.

"Do you trust me, Esi?"

My gaze met his. "Yes, I do. Although I have a question. Why are we here?"

"Great, so let's go inside and you'll find out."

He opens the car door for me and holds my hand as we enter the building. In the distance I hear music, and it sounds like "My Boo" by Usher ft. Alicia Keys. That's when it dawns on me. *Oh my God, this man is asking me to be his girlfriend. Wow, this is really happening.* As we walk deeper into the venue, I see pictures of us all around. Then I see a heart-shaped arch that has flowers with words in pink neon saying, "Will You Be My Girlfriend?"

"You know we've been going on dates, and I have been enjoying my time with you, Esi. From the moment we met, I knew you were special. I wanted to express my love for you and reassure you that I am not going anywhere. You mean so much to me. Will you be my girlfriend?"

Wow, this man cares so deeply about me. "Yes, I will. When did you plan all this?" I laugh because I can't believe my eyes.

"My heart is content. I had time to plan while you were away in Ghana. I am so happy you said yes. Was nervous you would reject me."

"I would never do that. You have been so kind and amazing to know."

"Likewise, I have one more thing to give you."

He pulls out a blue velvet box. "I want to show my commitment to this relationship and my intentions to marry you one day. Here is this promise ring."

It's a pink heart shaped ring. We kiss and hold hands while gazing at each other. It's a great end to the night. Months ago, I would've thought I'd never fall in love, but tonight, God has shined his light on me. He has taught me he'll never leave nor forsake me. That my wishes don't go unheard. Amadi drops me off at my apartment before heading home.

One of my nonnegotiable before we became official was no going to each others' homes. He respected my wishes and hasn't pushed further. I mentioned to him that I wanted to take this abstinence journey serious. It's been challenging but I feel the most at peace. Anyways, I'm on top of the moon tonight. God saw my tears and turned an unpleasant situation around for my good. If I didn't have faith before I definitely do now. *Ahhh, I cannot believe I am somebody's girlfriend.* That was so quick. God really works in his own timing and with speed at times. I can't contain my excitement. Each time I get the chance, I'm taking a glance at my ring. This is the moment I have always wished for. A kind, generous, and understanding man. A man that is honest and trustworthy, which I believe I found in Amadi.

The next morning, I receive a call from my mom, which isn't out of the ordinary. *I just hope she didn't have one of those dreams again.* Then she'll really pester me about my love life. I should tell her first, so she can hear from the source. "Hello Mommy, how are you?"

"I am doing good. Just taking things one day at a time by God's grace. So, what is new?"

"Well, you might not believe this, but I have a boyfriend now. Amadi asked me in a grand way. He rented a space for us and everything."

"I am so happy to hear this. Wa ma makoma nto me yam. You have given me peace of mind."

"Ahh, Mommy, why did you say that?"

"I want what is best for you, Esi. You are my only daughter that isn't married yet. I want to see you with the right man of God, and he is granting my prayers."

"Yes, he is doing a good thing within my life. Marriage, as you know, isn't the end all be all."

"Ehh, what do you mean by that, Esi? A woman needs companionship."

"Marriage is a blessing, but if it doesn't happen, life still goes on. You can still be fulfilled in other ways. Plus, you must have things going for yourself as a woman. Have you seen the dating market nowadays, it's a nightmare. Especially if you don't practice discernment."

"Now that you say that, it makes sense. I just want life to work out for you the way it has for your sisters."

"Mommy, I will be all right, and please don't compare me to my siblings. I am my own person. You don't need to worry. Everything works out in the end."

"Sorry, my dear. I just care about you so much and want to see you shine. I hope that man in your life is treating you well."

"I know you do, and I appreciate that about you. Yes, he is treating me better than any guy has before. He even got me a promise ring."

"Sa abrantɛɛ wei yɛ serious. Isn't a promise ring a commitment that he might marry you one day?"

Hearing my mom say that makes me chuckle because of how dramatic she's being. "Yes, it is, and that he will stay faithful to me. I hope one day I can get married, but for now, I just want to enjoy my life with this newfound love."

"That's awesome. When can we meet this guy?"

"Soon, he's the best man for Zuhrah and Tobenna's wedding."

"I can't wait. Oh, my daughter, I'm so happy."

We talked about the bridal shower coming up and the plans for that. The bridal shower planning is going well. We just need to attend the event. Everything was sorted out in advance. I'm worried things might go awry, because sometimes wedding planning can get overwhelming, but I'm grateful for the lovely ladies in the bridal party. My mom and I end the call after two hours. Not less than thirty minutes later, I get messages flooding my phone from the family group chat. Upon further inspection, it's my sisters saying how happy they were for me. *Mommy did not waste time spilling the tea to the whole family.* Gabrielle, Anastasia, and Ivy had similar reactions. Apart from being elated, they also prayed that I would be married soon. *Here we go again with the marriage thing.* Rolling my eyes as I read the messages. I will get married if it is the Lord's will for my life. I have no doubt I will. However, it is not my main concern anymore. Like the saying Que Sera Sera, whatever will be will be.

Fast forward a week later, and we are having the bridal shower. The theme of the shower is tea party with shades of pink. We have a variety of food from finger foods, desserts, and African food. The food was catered by a local African restaurant and a bakery. The bridal party had arrived early to decorate the place. The inspiration for the venue was English rose tearoom. We had everything set up from the floral décor to the shades of pink at every table. All the ladies who attended adhere to the dress code. My outfit is a halter neck corset waist styled midi dress with pleats. It's a hot pink color. I also wear a head piece to bring the look together. All the guests in attendance look amazing. A time was had. Zuhrah comes in looking magnificent. She's shocked by all the love she's receiving. Every woman she knows is in attendance, which she later tells me warmed her heart. She wears all white, of course. More specifically, she has on an off-the-shoulder lace detailed dress with a head piece and gloves, plus cute heels. She has on pearl jewelry to match. We play so many games. One involves making and modeling a wedding dress using paper towels. It's so much fun.

The best part of the day is when Tobenna comes in with different shades of pink flowers and a gift for Zuhrah. Enthusiasm and joy filled her soul as she danced with her man. She feels loved and appreciated this day. People that are married give the couple marital advice. Zuhrah's mom gives them advice.

"Always give one another grace when you make a mistake in marriage. Remember that this is a lifetime partnership and union that God has created for you. Never forget that. Do not let others interfere with your marriage because it will cause lots of fights and disagreements. Settle your matters together and consult wise counsel. You are supposed to love one another with Christ at the center."

It's beautifully said.

The food tastes as good as it appears. Everyone has a wonderful time just bonding and celebrating Zuhrah and Tobenna. I can tell she's having an exciting time from her facial expressions and the fact that she's smiling every chance she gets. Everyone takes pictures with the bride and groom. It's time consuming towards the end. This warms my heart and gives me hope for the future. After the celebration it's time to clean up. Well, the bridal party does while we usher people out of the venue. It isn't too tedious cleaning since there are a lot of us that are helping. When everything is finished, I get a ride with my mom while my sisters go on their way. She won't stop pestering me about my relationship with Amadi and when she'll get to meet him.

"Mom, I thought we discussed this already. You'll meet him soon at Zuhrah's wedding."

"I know, but I am so hopeful that one day you'll get married soon. You know it's not good for man to be alone."

"Mommy, I am well aware, but I just became a girlfriend, so marriage will take time. Plus, you know what happened when I tried to push marriage on a guy."

"I know my darling, but this is different. Your relationship will end in marriage, and it will be successful. Do you hear me?"

"Yes, from your lips to God's ears." *Part of me knows what she saying is true, but I don't want heartbreak again, so I am taking it easy.* I arrive at my home safely and wish my mom safe travels. By time I check my phone, I have messages from Amadi.

AMADI:

Hey babe, hoping you are well. I know you have been at the bridal shower. Wish I could see your beautiful face. How did it go?

ESI:

It was wonderful being surrounded by love. Aww, I also wish I could see you, handsome. But at least we have the wedding to look forward to and many more dates.

AMADI:

That is great to know. More time together is what I look forward to. Was my homeboy crying?

ESI:

I look forward to seeing you. He was smiling from ear to ear. He is saving the crying for the wedding when she walks down the aisle. That is my honest guess.

AMADI:

I figure as much. They are in love. Ain't nothing coming between them. Tobenna is going to shed tears, I think as well.

ESI:

Tell me about it. Zuhrah has not talked so highly of any man since she met him. Also, tell me why my mom is inquiring about meeting you.

AMADI:

Really? Likewise, when it comes to Tobenna. He loves Zuhrah ain't no joke. Wow, your mom wants to meet me so soon? I guess I have to be on my best behavior. I'd be delighted to meet your family. They're attending the wedding, right?

ESI:

Yes, they all are coming. My mom even inquired about marriage. Like, slow down, lady. Don't worry, my family will love you.

AMADI:

WOW, she's already hinting at marriage huh. I mean there's no doubt we'll get married. We just need to take our time.

ESI:

You're so sure. How do you know?

AMADI:

I know because I love you. I'm madly in love with you.

ESI:

Well, that shut me up. I have nothing left to say. I love you too. Great to know we mutually feel this way.

AMADI:

> I wouldn't say this if I didn't mean it. You are mine and I want to spend forever getting to explore the layers of you.

ESI:

> You're so sweet.

AMADI:

> Isn't that why you love me? My parents also want to meet the woman whose placed a permanent smile on my face.

ESI:

> Why yes! And I can't believe I will get to meet your parents. I wish you had siblings, because I'd get along well with them.

AMADI:

> I know. I'm solo around here, but that's okay because I never feel alone.

To think I almost did not allow this love into my life because of my past. When I thought about God showing me how good it will get, I did not imagine this. Enough of me gushing over my man. What am I going to do about meeting his parents? I have no doubt they will like me, but usually the first time is nerve-wracking. I don't want to make a fool of myself. Everything will turn out fine. I whisper to myself, *I hope.* I get ready to sleep and snuggle in my bed. Happy that I won't have work for a few more days until after the wedding. I am admiring pictures of my dress and imagining my gele/duku complementing my outfit along with my accessories.

The bridesmaids have been talking about doing more dance rehearsals before the big day. The groomsmen have their own system going on, but we'll come together to dance in pairs during the white wedding. I know that since Amadi and I play pivotal roles, we will be paired together. Me being the maid of honor and him being the best man. Not sure who knows that we are dating, but they will find out real soon. The stress of it all is getting worse, but I would do it again to see my friend happy. This will be a three-day affair. The traditional wedding will be the first week in September on a Friday, and the white wedding will be the following day. Then it will be the thanksgiving ceremony on Sunday welcoming the new couple. Eventually, I fall asleep having dozed off after replying to my love.

Life gets better when you let go of controlling every aspect of it and let the creator God take the driver's seat. As long as you are a good person, nothing the enemy throws your way will prosper. This is the thought I have in mind whilst I'm out with my siblings. Today, we decided to meet up and chat at a local frozen yogurt shop. You know I haven't really been the type to enjoy hanging out with family. The hurt they have caused me when I was younger was enough for me to distance myself. Today feels different. It's the first time we're all together. No competition, no arguments, and no unnecessary drama. Just quality time being spent.

"So, Esi, what's going on in your love life?" Gabrielle said.

My sisters Anastasia and Ivy have their eyes glued on me like a hawk. All I can do is nervously laugh.

Where should I start? "My love life is going well ever since I met Amadi. He's a breath of fresh air."

"Okay, that sounds promising. When are we going to meet to this fine fellow?" Ivy chimes in.

"He's a part of the wedding party, so I will introduce him then. For now, I can show you a picture of him." I show them his picture, which makes them smile.

"He's handsome, girl. Oh, and looks like he has a dimple."

They begin singing the chorus to "Simple" by Bradez.

"I hope he's treating you right and not like those other men who shall not be named."

It wouldn't be Anastasia if she did not bring her sassy personality with her.

"Yes, he's treating me better than anyone I've dated in the past. I don't need to prove my worth with him he sees it."

"Our little sister has found love. How sweet. We're all so elated that God gave you a partner that loves you," Gabrielle said.

"Thank you, girls." I shake my head in agreement with what was said.

The rest of the time, my sisters are giving me advice. Although it's nice, I grow overwhelmed. My love life is something I want to protect, being that the past men haven't worked out. I will cherish this experience and remain lowkey for now. The last time I let my sisters intervene, it ended in heartbreak, but it did lead me to Amadi, so that was a plus. I have long since forgiven Gabrielle for that experience. The advice is much needed, and I knew it's coming from the heart.

"How's your pregnancy going, Anastasia?" I inquire.

"By God's grace, I'm doing fine, I should be due any day now. My due date is sometime in September or early October, but you know that babies come on their own timing. We shall see."

"Can't wait to be an auntie again. I'm definitely going to be the cool one," I say with a laugh.

"Nah, we all know I'm the better auntie," Ivy says. We all start cracking up with laughter.

Afterwards, we walk around the mall strip and do a little shopping. I buy a pair of shoes that will complement my dress for Zuhrah's big day. It's a gold strapped heel, and it's gorgeous. Everyone has their outfit and accessories ready to go. It's a great bonding experience and really brings us together as a family. Shortly after that, I go home and reflected on my day. My sisters and I really have come a long way, and I will forever be thankful. That shows growth on our end. Our parents would be incredibly surprised. They used to yell at us for fighting with each other back in the day. Those are times I do not want to ever experience again if I have to.

Days later, and I am enjoying dating Amadi. We really mesh well, and I can't imagine not having him by my side. I'm pleased to announce I meet his parents before the ceremony. Amadi takes me to his parents' house. It's a nice brownstone home in New Jersey. I'm nervous at first, but can you believe his parents love me? Mama Damilare is grilling Amadi about marriage. But he stays calm and collected.

"So, my son, when are you going to get married to this beautiful woman? You know you're my only child and I need grandkids."

"Ah Ah, Mommy, it will happen before you know it. I am glad you love Esi."

"Please make it fast, you know I'm getting old. How can I not love

Esi? She's the first woman you've brought to meet us. This means you're serious about one another."

"Mommy, that's because she's someone very special to me."

As he says this, he looks over at me, causing butterflies in my stomach.

"What matters to me is that you are happy, Amadi," his dad adds.

"I seriously am happy, can't you see?"

"I have one question for Esi. How do you feel about my son?"

Before I answer, I'm taking in my surroundings. "I must say that I care deeply about Amadi and wish he came in my life sooner."

Papa Damilare lets out a laugh that makes us all bust out laughing.

"That's all I needed to hear. Amadi, you have a good woman right here, don't take her for granted."

He shakes his head and says, "Yes, Dad."

The rest of the day is amazing, with delicious food and amazing company. It's my first time eating Nigerian jollof and fried rice with chicken stew and may I say, she put her best foot forward. I feel loved today, and I believe Amadi and I are moving in the right direction.

"Today is Friday, that means the wedding is a week away," Zuhrah says while on the phone.

"How is the bride-to-be feeling?"

"I am so nervous that things will go wrong that day. Thanks for getting my nerves going," she says sarcastically.

"I'm sorry, I just wanted to make sure you're all right. If there's anything I can do, please let me know."

"It's not your fault, weddings are stressful and anxiety inducing. I appreciate you thus far. You've been a big help."

"No problem, I completely understand, girl. Are you spilling the deets on your honeymoon getaway?"

"Yes, we have. We finalized it last month. Babe surprised me with tickets to the Maldives." She lets out a shriek after speaking.

"Wow Zuhrah, I'm so happy for you."

"Thanks so much, girl. So, tell me how's things going in your life?"

"Amadi and I are officially together, and I met his parents."

There is a silent pause before Zuhrah says something. "OH MY GOSH Esi! This is exciting news. Why didn't you tell me sooner?"

"I mean, I was trying to take it all in and I forgot."

"Please tell me he made you feel special."

"Yes, he did. It was an intimate moment with all our pictures of us together and a sign asking me to be his girlfriend. If he could do this for me, imagine him asking me to be his wife."

"I love to hear your enthusiasm, and don't worry, at the right time, that will happen and knowing him, it will be a grand gesture."

"Thanks, I have been through so much. I just want to be happy."

"You are working your way to being happier than ever. Don't wait for anyone to shift your emotions. You create that life for yourself."

"I needed to hear that. Thanks, sis."

"No problem. How did it go meeting his parents?"

"It was interesting, to say the least. They love me so much and I can see us building a bond. They might like me more than Amadi," I say with a chuckle.

"That is a good sign. If you can win the parents over, you have won in life."

"This is a good feeling to be liked by the parents. You know how African parents can be difficult at times."

"That is true. If they don't like you, forget about it."

"One of the reasons I was scared at first. We thank God, they love me."

The rest of the conversation is spent talking about the wedding and planning our last rehearsal.

Fast forward to the rehearsals, and I'm getting more antsy thinking about our appearance and how we'll coordinate at the wedding. Gisella is the one who choreographed the whole dance. She is better than me because getting all the girls to dance is a job in itself.

"All right, everyone, let us take it from the top. And a one, two, three, let's go." Gisella said aloud.

The music choice is "My Darlin'" by Tiwa Savage. The dance routine is us moving from side to side with our fans as we dance coming inside the venue and then splitting into two single-formed lines shaking the fan as Zuhrah dances in with the Adowa dancers. We're paired and dance facing each other, swaying our hips. Then we move forward, dancing to the opposite side and switching spots.

Finally, we form a circle around our bride while she dances in the middle. We do the dance moves perfectly and have the handheld fans to complete the dance. I can imagine it now. Once we put on our outfits, hair, makeup, and accessories, everything will come together. We practice the entrance at least three times with Zuhrah. Then we transition into the partner dances with the guys, who come in two hours later.

"We all know the order in which we are going in the venue right? Please partner up and practice your routine," Gisella says.

We nod our heads and get to practicing.

"We meet again, Esi," Amadi whispers. For whatever reason, I begin laughing.

"Aww, sounds like you miss me already."

He shrugs his shoulders before saying, "Hey what can I say, I do."

"Come on, let's show our moves, we're up next."

"As you wish, my forever lady."

The song we chose is "Enjoyment" by Kidi, which begins playing and we know exactly what to do. We do our handshake before starting the dance. I start first, leading the way before Amadi comes in, spraying dollars on me. I did pilolo followed by the zibit dance. He does his own version of azonto dance moves with incorporation of leg work, and we join to dance freestyle. He spins me around before the music cuts off.

I feel the chemistry between us on the dance floor. We practice our entrance at least two more times before stopping for the day. Amadi drives me to get my hair done, since the wedding is the next day.

"How do you feel now that we have practiced our dance routine?" Amadi asks.

"I feel great. I mean, look, we did well. I have you to thank for that, my love." I plant a kiss on his lips, which makes him smile.

"Thanks babe, you know how to make my head swell. Let's take you to the salon."

"Right now, it's 1:30 pm. I have enough time to get to my appointment at 2:15 pm."

"Let's get going."

I arrive to my destination with only fifteen minutes to spare. I give

Amadi a hug and kiss before entering the shop. My stylist Ness will get my hair all the way together.

"Hello, Esi, I'm so glad to see you. Please sit down on the chair." I greet her and do as she request.

"I have not seen you in a long time. Where have you been?"

"I have been embracing my natural hair more."

"Oh, I see. What style we have for today?"

I open my phone and show her the style. Zuhrah wanted all of us to wear either a bun or ponytail. Knowing me, I'm extra, I am going for a swoop bang with a Barbie ponytail.

"Ooo, Esi, this hair will look great on you. You are in for a treat."

Ness hooks my hair up. I love the look so much, I have to do a double take in the mirror. Amadi is busy doing last minute things, so I decide to take a car service home. I send him a selfie of me. He does not hesitate to love the message and text, *I cannot wait to see you tomorrow.* I make sure to wrap my hair in a scarf and bonnet before heading to bed. I know it was early, but this three-day affair will tire me out.

Chapter Seven

AYEFRO DONDOO (WEDDING BELLS)

THE PHOTOGRAPHER AND VIDEOGRAPHER DO A SPECTACULAR JOB. They stay patient while we change looks. We go from wearing bridal robes to putting on our kente clothes. The cloth we have is a pink champagne color which are in unique styles. The star of the show has so many poses planned, which are executed beautifully. Makeup takes a while but there's perfection in waiting. Believe me when I say my ego is on a ten with this face beat. I can say Zuhrah really outdid herself; she gave each of the bridal party gifts that match our personalities. She got me a Fujifilm Instax smartphone printer so I can take pictures for memories and a scrapbook with some stickers. Along with smell-good items. Everyone loves their gifts. It's time for Zuhrah and her hubby to exchange gifts as well. I take on the responsibility of delivering the items to the groom. As soon as I reach toward the men's hotel suite, I meet Amadi coming towards, me bearing gifts for Zuhrah.

"Esi, I am lost for words, you look so gorgeous. They sent you to give Tobenna his gift?"

"Thank you so much, and I volunteered myself, if you can say that."

"The pleasure is mine. You are the woman of my dreams."

Esi, breathe. This man is making me feel shy suddenly. What is going on? All I could do was play it cool by saying, "You are so blessed to have me in your world."

Looking deeply in my eyes, he flashes me a smile. Then, he took my hand and kisses it before walking off. *This man thinks he can confuse me with his charm.* I let out a playful laugh and suck my teeth. I knock on the door, and the groomsmen greet me. There are six groomsmen in total. The first one is Asante, then Desmond, Femi, Adom, Nabil, and finally my man Amadi. Desmond is the one who lets me in. He is a tall, brown-skinned man with a bald head and full beard. He is Tobenna's older brother.

"Aye, it is Esi, and she came with some gifts," Desmond said aloud over the music playing.

"Hello, I am here to drop off Tobenna's gift from the Missus."

"Thank you so much, my friend. Wonder what it could be. It is packaged so nicely."

"No problem."

"My brother, open it and find out," Femi says.

Tobenna is about to open the gifts when he tells me this. "Before you go, can you tell Zuhrah I appreciate and love the time and effort she put into these gifts?"

"Will do."

He carefully opens the gifts and sees Louis Vuitton branding. He says, "Wow, my babe has class. Talk to me nice. The way she loves me no be small."

Everyone busts out in laughter. He opens the smaller box, and it is a gold Rolex watch. He's filled with joy. As I walk back to the bridal suite, I feel a sense of peace. Thinking that one day, this will be me. I'm so distracted by my thoughts, I don't notice Amadi. His voice snaps me out of my daydream.

"Did Tobenna like his gifts?"

"Yes, you should have seen his reaction—so hilarious. What about Zuhrah?"

"Man, that would have been a sight to see. Zuhrah was a ball of energy. She also loved her gifts."

"That's nice. I'll find out what he got her in a moment."

As soon as I say that, his phone buzzes, which distracts him for a bit. "Yeah, the two love birds really matched each other's energy with these gifts. I will see you later, they have me doing something right now. I just cannot get over how good you look."

He quickly left shortly after. I enter the suite, and everyone is filled with joy. Zuhrah is admiring her gifts, which happen to be a silver jewelry set, Pandora bracelet with charms, and a Coach Tabby shoulder bag in pink. We even were able to capture her mother praying over her marriage.

Fast forward to the bride and groom's first look. The whole aspect felt wholesome. Zuhrah is videoed coming downstairs and tapping her man to reveal her look. The kente is flattering on her body. She wears an all-pink off-the-shoulder kente dress with beading, and it has adinkra symbols throughout it. Her hair is a deep side part with curls. Her makeup is stunning; she really looks like a celebrity. Get into the details on her fan. It has the symbol gye nyame and Bamidele is written across. Tobenna takes one look at her and is surprised.

"Babe, you look so amazing. I must do a double take. Everyone should be cheering because you are a ten out of ten."

"You are so sweet, my love," Zuhrah responds as she turned herself around. When you find your match, you glow different.

Love is beautiful, but it alone can't sustain a relationship. The two people must have things going for themselves to make it work. The individuals need to make a commitment to stay with each other even during the tough times. That is how you know the feelings are real. We take a few pictures together as an entourage before heading to the venue in Queens. We are running on time, surprisingly. The guys go in first while we wait in the party bus for our queue to enter. I wish I could see how their dance turned out. "I remember Amadi telling me the song is "4Life" by Kidi, and a mix of other afrobeats songs. It feels like ages until an Auntie came in, telling us we could come inside. Lining up like we had rehearsed took us a minute. That is when we heard "Here Comes the Bride!" then the "My Darlin'" song starts to play. We dance our way in the hall with our choreography capturing the eyes of many. The real applause is when Zuhrah dances in with the Adowa dancers. Zuhrah has her moment in the middle as we form a circle around her. I'm so in-tune with the music playing.

All of us migrate to the side and take our reserved seats. The emcee transitions us to the next aspect of the wedding along with the Twi interpreter. It's important to Zuhrah that people understand what was going on. Especially the non-Twi speakers. The groom goes over to the bride's section to look for Zuhrah. She has her fan covering her face.

The emcee asks, "Is this the lady you want to marry?"

"Yes, she is the one," Tobenna says.

He slowly lowers the fan, and she starts to smile at him. The rest of the time is spent explaining the customs of Ghana and the importance of it all. The moment we're all waiting for is the interaction between Zuhrah and her father. Her dad is saying to her how he raised her 'til this point. He expresses admiration for her being a good child. Even though she's outspoken, it has brought her much success in life.

Finally, he asks her the famous lines three times: "Yen gye nnɔɔma?" This was to make sure she is serious about the marriage.

"Daddy," she says with a chuckle. "Aane mo'n gye nnɔɔma. sɛ woannye nneɛma yi a obiara endidi nnɛ" Zuhrah said.

The translator interprets what she says and adds, "She is a lover girl, indeed."

Everyone lets out a big aye. Pastor Richard brings the couple to the front to officiate the wedding and pray for them. Once that's done, it's time for Zuhrah and Tobenna to wear their Nigerian garments. I'm shocked that she changed more than once, but knowing her, she wants to go big. The emcee announces the latest couple, and they make their entrance. As they walk inside, adowa dancers lead the way. Zuhrah wants to have bits and pieces of her culture meshed in the wedding. They dance to the song "Kelewele" by Smallgod ft Joeboy. Zuhrah's gele is tied nicely and paired with her gold dress that steals the show. They make their way onto the floor and dance while being sprayed with money. Everyone gets out of their seats and are mingling with one another.

During this time, I notice my family. I look for Amadi and whisper in his ear, "Hey, I would really like to introduce you to my family. They're near the left-hand side."

"Sure, let's go," he says with no hesitation.

My family is accepting of Amadi. It warms my heart to see this interaction. My dad is the first to hug him, which is interesting, because he doesn't like many people.

"So, this is Amadi. The man that has caught my daughter's attention. How are you?"

"I'm good. I'm pleased to meet you. Are we all having a fun time?" Amadi says.

My mom chimes in, saying, "I believe so. Everything was done perfectly. You are so respectful and nice. May God bless you, my son."

My sisters are smiling so much at the both of us. It wouldn't be my sisters if at least one of them didn't say something.

Ivy opens her mouth to say, "Amadi what are your plans with Esi?" Anastasia and Gabrielle nod their heads in agreement. My mom shoots her a look.

"What? I'm simply curious, is all."

Amadi, working well under pressure, does not fold regarding this question.

"I care so deeply for Esi, and I plan on building forever with her. She makes life easier with her presence. I would not do anything to break what we have built together. I hope that answers your question."

Aww, how sweet. I could cry right now.

"Yes, it does. You have a great head on your shoulders. Wishing you two the best." Everyone agrees with Ivy.

That has to be a good sign. right? We have duties to attend to, so we tell them goodbye and join the wedding party. A portion of the wedding is reserved for picture taking, which feels like forever. The rest of the time at the wedding is spent eating Ghanaian and Nigerian dishes, from eba and egusi to light soup and fufu. Not to mention waakye, fried rice, and jollof with assorted meat. We dance until it's time to leave.

We return to the hotel suite, get unready and into pajamas. Despite Zuhrah and Tobenna being married, they are advised to sleep separately tonight until the next day. The night ends early due to exhaustion. The next morning, we get up bright and early. The makeup artist's hands are gifted. I feel great in my rose gold dress. We take videos and pictures. We get to see Zuhrah's look first. Our reactions are priceless. She has a beaded appliqué dress which is fitted at the top and flares out. She has a long train. She has a sultry makeup look, and her hair is styled in a bridal bun with a 3D-braided flower in the back. She got her dress made by a popular Nigerian designer with the help of her mother-in-law. The pastor's wife Emilia, along with her mom, pray for Zuhrah. Due to time restrictions, the couple's first look will be at the church when she walks down the aisle. I didn't see the groomsmen until we arrive at the church. Then, one by one, we each pair up and walk.

The moment we've been waiting for has come. Zuhrah finally walks down the aisle with her dad. I look over at Tobenna and he's shedding tears. It's expected from him. He wears his heart on his sleeve when it comes to her. Luckily, Amadi is prepared and passes a tissue. Zuhrah walks to the midpoint. Tobenna walks over to take her hand from his father-in-law. Pastor Richard from the day before is officiating the wedding today. The couple exchanges vows like they had planned. Tobenna starts first.

"Zuhrah, what can I say. You have been the best person for me. You've seen me at my best and worst, but still chose to love me. We're the perfect fit for each other. Loving you has been the best choice I've made. I will keep loving you 'til the end."

Zuhrah says her vows.

"My love, I have gotten to know you over these past two years, and it has been an amazing journey. I find new ways of loving you all over again. You're my best friend and I couldn't imagine doing life without you. Please keep being the man I fell in love with. You're one of the most amazing people I've gotten to know. I'm ready to do forever with you."

I can tell they put thought into their vows. Short, sweet, and to the point. Shortly after, the pastor takes over and formally announces them husband and wife. They kiss, which sends the congregation in a frenzy. I can hear people saying, "Kiss her again." We transition into prayer and praise. The time flies by and before I know it, we're at the venue.

Our time to shine. Amadi and I scatter that dance floor with our moves. garnering praise from the crowd. As soon as he sprays me with dollars, I'm filled with enthusiasm. Once Zuhrah and Tobenna come, everyone's eyes are glued on them. You can feel the chemistry between the love birds. The rest of the time is spent partying and participating in the festivities. I sneak out to get some pictures of myself and Amadi for memories. He says to me, "Who would have thought we'd be in love?" He then kisses my cheek.

I look at him and smile. Falling in love after heartbreak has been very interesting. Some people never fall in love again, while some move on fast. My journey has been met with hardship, but now I feel like I can finally breathe.

"Aww, I didn't know you two were together?"

I turn around and see Aiysha, which makes me giggle. All I say is, "Yes, we are dating."

"I am so happy for you both. I can see the chemistry you both have. It's lovely to see."

We say in unison, "Thank you!"

I guess the cat's out the bag. The day ends pretty late. Before I know it, we're singing praises at church the next morning and welcoming the latest couple in town. The last thing that the pastor says that I remember is, "Yesu Kristo ɔbɛdi w'akyi daa," and I really internalize it. Life has taught me to accept love and to be cheerful for others when their moment comes. God will make your moment come when the time is ready. You won't have to beg to be chosen. Things will just flow naturally towards you. Having ill will for others shows you have not healed. This journey called life will give you the lessons you need to learn at the appropriate time.

"You will make the most beautiful bride one day," Amadi says to me, with his eyes glistening as we walk to his car.

"Oh, really? You throwing hints my way?"

"I wouldn't say it if I wasn't certain, it would be true."

"Aww, you love me."

He cups my face with his hand and gives me a kiss. I go silent, unable to speak.

"I can show you better than I can tell you. From the moment I met you, I knew you were special. Would not change a thing about you."

"What is a girl supposed to say now? You have left me speechless."

"I do have a question for you, though."

"Ask away, my love."

"What happened in your past relationship that caused it to end? I know I should've asked you this in the beginning, but better late than never, right?"

Why does he want to know about my past?

I clear my throat and let out a sigh before speaking.

"Long before we met, and before the last guy I briefly dated, I was in a committed relationship with a guy named Seth. It ended because I was expecting marriage and that was not where he was at mentally. He would tell me I was stressing him out and eventually we broke up. It shattered my hopes of finding love again, but I guess God works in mysterious ways."

"I'm sorry you had to experience that. However, I am happy because those experiences led you to me."

"I love you and I'm so grateful you came in just the nick of time."

I thought about pushing Amadi away multiple times, but something about him felt safe. For the first time in a long time, I feel like I can let my guard down.

"Two hearts have found each other when they least expected it."

"You are right about that. Since we're being vulnerable, it's my turn to ask. What happened in your last relationship that caused it to end?"

"My ex and I weren't a good fit. We always argued and it was recipe for disaster. I can't blame her for everything though, I was immature. I learned my lesson after that time in my life."

"I like how you're introspective about your own faults. Not too many people are."

"All I can say is I've grown. I mean, I am a lover boy which can be a bit off-putting for some people."

"Well, Mr. Loverboy has met his match. On another note, do you think we've helped each other in this relationship?"

He just laughs and says, "Of course, Esi. You have shown me what love really is. It's constantly sacrificing for one another and watching each other grow as individuals. I am the happiest when I'm with you."

"I am glad to know we see the best in each other."

This is the kind of relationship I have subconsciously wanted that I did not know I needed. People always say love finds you when you stop looking. Whether you go searching for it or not doesn't change the outcome. What's meant to be will be. I have met counterfeits posing as the real thing. Those experiences left scars, but I am learning to patch things back together again. Accepting love is the first step. The healing journey after heartbreak is met with grieving the life I thought I wanted for something better. All this while I have been settling, thinking I deserved constant disrespect. Not knowing there was a life of gentleness awaiting me.

Our conversation delves deeper on what we can do to better our relationship. We agree to not let the day end without speaking about our feelings if one of us is upset. That is reasonable, because anger has physiological effects on the body if you let the emotion fester. This is the first time I feel heard in a relationship. It's amazing to be with someone who listens to understand and not just respond. Most people argue and talk over each other with no clear resolution. This is the type of behavior I accepted in the past. I'm glad that's not me anymore. *Have I found my match? I can't escape this feeling that we are meant to be. Like the saying that God puts people in our path the time we need them the most.* This night shows me I can let my walls down for once.

Chapter Eight

BUNDLE OF JOY

WHAT A WHIRLWIND OF EMOTIONS TODAY. ANASTASIA FINALLY GAVE birth to a healthy baby boy a few days ago. I feel grateful in this moment because I get to visit her with my family, and we bonded. She is still recovering, but she looks good despite all the pain. They decided to name baby Danso Nathaniel. What a nice name. It suits him well. I get to hold him, and he looks so precious from his little hands to his little toes. I am about to leave having baby fever. It was fun being around my family. Especially seeing my nieces and nephews brings immense joy to my heart. We eat some delicious food that sends my taste buds into overload. I forget how much I miss my mom's cooking, especially her meat pie and waakye with stew. I will take some to go. Living alone, I hardly ever cook meals for myself that's not quick and meal-prepped. I love the peace that comes with living on my own.

"I can't wait for it to be your turn, Esi," my mom says.

"My turn for what?" I say in a curious tone.

"I can't wait for you and Amadi to tie the knot and give me grand-children."

"Mom, why must you always bring this up any chance you get?" Ivy says.

"Well, I just want to see my last born married and living her life."

Everyone just starts shaking their heads.

"Mommy, we are taking our time to get to know each other. I have no doubt that he'll pop the question. It's just a matter of patience. You remember what happened when I rushed someone concerning marriage. Right?"

"I know very well. But that guy did not have common sense to see what was right for him. Seth put up a good front, but like they say, it doesn't last for long."

"You're right about the lack of common sense part, but it led me to finding better."

"You found better indeed, but I still worry about you."

"I don't want you to, because I will be okay regardless of how this relationship turns out."

"Hey, don't say that. My dear, think positive."

I have been thinking about my future and how I'll be as a wife and mom. The thought of that makes me nervous. It brings me back to Zuhrah's thanksgiving ceremony when Amadi told me I'd make a beau-tiful bride. Although he loves me, it's difficult to believe anyone could love me at times. I know I have been on a journey of self-love and acceptance, but some days are harder than others. I mean, being a plus-sized girly isn't easy. People aren't forgiving when you're bigger than society's standards. They judge, make fun, and belittle. This brings me into another thought. What if I am not a good wife and end up divorced, leaving me a single mom? Not saying that I haven't seen successful single mothers, but it does take a village to raise a child. It's thoughts like this that might leave me single.

Snap out of it, girl! That's negative thinking, which we do not need in our lives. You have a man who loves you. You're amazing to get to know and be in love with. All that insecurity is for the birds.

Every day has felt long for the past month. I guess me getting back into my routine of being at work has really thrown me off. I am so tired all the time. Zuhrah told me to take it easy and get more sleep. Speaking of her, she came back from her trip to the Maldives.

"Hey Esi, how have you been? I am calling to thank you for being a wonderful maid of honor. You're my girl, and I love you."

"You are so welcome, it was a pleasure supporting you on your big day. Sis, I have been taking your advice and working on getting more sleep and adjusting my stress levels. Also, Anastasia gave birth to a healthy boy. It's taking a while to adhere to my regular schedule, but other than that, I'm good. What about you?"

"What!? That's amazing, what's the baby's name? I hope you can fix your sleep patterns, but it's hard since you had the summer off from work. I have been doing good. I mean I'm a wife now, so it's been a huge learning curve. Had to move my things into a new apartment. Living with a man is quite interesting to say the least."

"She named her son Nathaniel. I see, and living with a man is something I have to brace myself for."

"Wonderful, I will have to call her soon. Also, don't get me wrong, it's amazing to finally live with your partner, but sometimes you just need your alone time as well."

"That's very true, which is why you need to have your own motion. Your whole identity shouldn't be tied to you being in a relationship."

"Exactly. Anyways, how's your relationship going with Amadi?"

"Things between us are amazing. I met his parents and they're nice people. My family loves him and wants us to get married already." I roll my eyes after saying that.

"This is great news. To think you were down in your feelings about that other guy only to find Amadi. Things always change for the better. Do not pay your family any mind, they're just excited to see you be loved properly."

"I know, I know, he came at the right time. Even though I wanted to resist the connection at first."

"It is okay, you were going through a lot emotionally. Very understandable. Always remember you are worthy of being loved romantically and platonically."

"Thank you so much. Sometimes, I feel so insecure."

"Insecurities happen to the best of us. It's how we react to them that matters. You cannot let that defeat you."

Tears start to form in my eyes hearing this, because this is what I need to hear. She saw right through me.

We talk for about an hour, which felt longer, but when the conversation becomes too good, you lose track of time. It's moments like this that I'm grateful for the friendship I have with Zuhrah. She has seen me through it all and still chose to be my friend. Not too many people can have a friend that uplifts, encourages, and helps you through challenging times. I could've run to my family in the past. However, some things my family just doesn't understand. I don't think they ever will, in all honesty. They are all so obsessed with the idea of me getting married that they can't see anything else. My life aspirations are much more than being someone's partner. I want to be the best speech pathologist for my students and get a higher paying job for my level of experience. As well as be the most in-shape I can be for myself and become a homeowner. My life is going to be what I make of it.

What's hurting me is that I am capable of greatness, but things haven't quite aligned for me lately, but as I stated before, life is what you make of it. I am hardworking and determined, which has gotten me far. I have no doubt that I'll have a great future. Work is getting exhausting, adjusting back to it, and the work demands have me in search of another one with a higher salary. I love what I do, but feel I've overstayed my course at this job. I will miss the environment, including some of my coworkers, but I know I need a change for the better. I know God wouldn't place this in my heart if it wasn't going to happen. Amadi has been very supportive. Always encouraging me to do what makes me content. He's a good person to have in my corner. Everything else will occur in its perfect timing, that I'm not worried about. I might not be where I want to be, but I'm certainly not anywhere I used to be. My life is leveling up for the better. As I'm thinking, I pick up my notebook and begin plotting my ideal life.

One where I am even more confident in my abilities. It dawns on me that taking little steps each day will get me there. I started to create what they call SMART goals. Each goal must be specific, measurable, attainable, relevant, and time bound. This is what I learned when I was in undergrad. It helped me a long way during my time in school, which made sense because I was more successful. I feel as though I'm on a roll with planning. I even decide to do a vision board with my old magazines to help me visualize everything. As well as my crafts kit with all the supplies needed to bring my ideas to life. I put the board on my bedroom wall, feeling empowered for change. I look at my board, thinking of ways to fulfill my dreams. I actively am in pursuit of a better life than the one I currently have. It's like a switch lit up in my mind.

Every day for the month in October, I do some small actionable steps towards a better me. I will exercise three times a week, which is a huge adjustment. I will even go with Amadi to the gym at least two of those times, and the other is spent following an at-home workout routine. What I hope for comes true; I secure a job for next school year with a $15,000 pay raise. The environment is conducive to my needs a speech therapist. God has done it again. I might not always understand why things occur in my life, but I know it all serves a purpose. Now that those events have passed, I have time to reflect. The very thing that was causing me pain was my steppingstone to greatness. If only I had known this sooner, I wouldn't have spent time living in self-doubt. The newer version of myself is thanks to a change in mindset. It could be Amadi's charm rubbing off on me, or the fact that being with him has made me realize my self-worth. *Thank you, Lord, for bringing him in my life.*

November and December, oh how I love you. Thanksgiving and Christmas are the best for me. It has made me understand the meaning of togetherness and family. The holidays used to bring upon sadness. Each year, I would wonder why I had the holiday blues. For the past two holidays, I wanted to be married and eventually start my own traditions with my newfound family. Since that never happened, I was left with my lonely thoughts of inadequacy. This year was the beginning of something different. Not only did Baby Nathaniel get to spend his first holiday in the world, but it's my first time meeting Amadi's extended family during Thanksgiving. They welcome me with open arms, which is heartwarming. I bring meat pie and bofrot that I made using my mother's recipe. They love it. The women in his family keep referring to me as *Omalicha*, which in Igbo translates to *beautiful*. The way it sweetens me when they say that you'd think I was a super model. The food is amazing. Thinking about it makes my mouth water. I have enough food to last me the following week after.

It's also the first of many experiences with Amadi. For Christmas, we exchange gifts at his condo in Jersey.

"Esi, I know the holidays haven't been the best for you in the past. I am willing to change that."

"You're so sweet. What did I do to deserve you?"

"Nothing, just simply being you is enough for me. I want to make you feel loved and supported during the holiday season."

"Thank you for considering my emotions. You mean so much to me."

This man loves me down. He bought me tons of gifts, and each was meaningful. My favorite has to be the Pandora bracelet with charms, and the heart locket necklace with a picture of us on inside. On the outside, *I Love You* is engraved. Words can't explain the intentionality that was put into each gift. I also give him presents, but I believe he takes the cake for best gift giver. He loves the painting I got of us together. He says, and I quote, "Babe, you did a fantastic job with this gift. I can't wait to hang this up."

He gives me the biggest bear hug and plants a kiss on my cheek. I love it when he gives me hugs, because it reminds me I'm loved. I am safe with him. Plus, chef's kiss, he smells so good. The cologne capsulates my nostrils with the fragrance of warm vanilla. We spend the whole time bonding with one another. I believe that we are moving towards the right direction. Who knows, I might be a Missus real soon. The thought of that scares me, but I'm very confident in my assumption. Each time we're together, I find new ways of loving him. It's one of life's greatest pleasures to be loved correctly. To have a firm foundation that's unshakable. That's the love we are all striving to attain. It's a miracle that I was able to find it.

The idea of life getting better for me is so surreal. I prayed for times like this. I am living in an answered prayer. Anyways, I am very excited for the new year and what it has in store. *New Year, show me how good it can get.* December 31ˢᵗ is tomorrow, and I am going to church with Amadi. It's a typical occurrence for us to attend church service to bring in the year. Although I haven't always been successful at times, I at least would watch the crossover service online. Another one of my goals is to trust God even through uncertainty. Often, I try to play the role of God in my life, not realizing that I'm human. What he can do, I cannot. Relying on my own strength can only take me so far. Dating Amadi has taught me life's greatest lesson, which is trusting in my maker. I don't have to know everything.

He always said, "Don't you trust that God lives in you?"

Amadi didn't know it then, but he was renewing my belief in Christ. That he can change things in his timing.

The next day, I get ready to go to Amadi's church in New Jersey. I opt for something comfortable that will keep me warm. I wear my reddish burgundy sweater dress with thermal leggings and knee-length black boots. The congregation is African, but it is a mix of mainly Nigerian and Ghanaians. My people we dey. That is something I used to hear often. You can tell everyone is on fire for the Lord, from the young ones all the way to the elders. A few hours into the crossover service and the vibes are excellent. The choir and praise dancers give me so much hope. The pastor instructs us to pray for the last thirty minutes before the new year. All the things I hope for to come true, I pray about. I want God to give me discernment concerning my next phase of life. I pray so much that tears trickle down my face. You know you have an impactful prayer session when you get emotional without any rhyme or reason. Amadi embraces me when he sees my tears. His hug is reassurance that I'm on the right path. Being with the right person most certainly brings out the best in you.

The clock strikes twelve, which sets everyone in a frenzy. Celebration breaks out, followed by dancing. Amadi and I are both dancing with one another. Everyone says happy new year to one another. Shortly after announcements, when we're about to leave, Amadi is greeted by the people he knows.

"Oh, wow, is that Amadi?" a manly voice says.

The man is shorter in stature with a low fade and medium brown skin. Amadi daps him up before introducing the man, whose name is Ivan.

"This is Esi, my girlfriend."

"Nice to meet you," I speak.

"So, this is the lovely woman you have been talking about."

"Yes, she's the one."

"Bro, I am so surprised. I didn't think you'd ever settle down."

"What can I say? I couldn't let an amazing person like Esi get away."

He wraps his arm around my shoulders in an endearing way. Ivan gives Amadi more accolades before turning to me and asking a question.

"Esi, what attracted you to my friend over here?"

"That is a great question. I'd say his confidence and his selflessness, not only towards me, but to others. He's an amazing individual, inside and out."

"How wonderful. My prayer is that you both stay together and get married. You have a good night and happy New Year."

"Amen," we both say in unison.

While we walk to Amadi's car, I turn to him and say, "This year will be monumental. I can feel a supernatural shift coming. I just have a feeling breakthroughs will occur."

"I think so too. From your lips to God's ears, my love." *Today is the start of something new.*

Chapter Nine

CELEBRATION TIME

LAST YEAR, I DIDN'T CELEBRATE MY BIRTHDAY AT ALL. THE thought of doing so brought me so much sadness. I had just broken up with my longtime partner of three years. My birthday being the following month on March 14th was my lowest point in life. No one knew why I didn't do anything spectacular for my 30th b-day. No one knew the sleepless nights or the times I felt behind in life due to this situation. Nobody asked, and so I suppressed my feelings and kept it to myself. I was a functionally depressed person. Apart from my close-knit circle of family and friends, no one wished me happy birthday. All the people I knew through my ex abandoned me when I needed them the most. Perfect timing, huh? I had hit rock bottom and trust me, I believed I'd stay there forever. I resented life for bringing such misery. Just when I was moving on, another imposter came into my life and did the same thing as the previous man. I understand that these experiences were meant to show me I deserved better. All this to say: a man that loves you will put in the work to show it. He won't be a counterfeit. You won't have to second guess his intentions with you.

Remember when I said this new year feels different? Not only does Amadi take me on a mini road trip to the Poconos, but he celebrates me the whole week of my 31st birthday. Every day, he gives me a gift that reminds him of me. One afternoon while I'm at work, he delivers a bouquet of pink flowers in cute packaging with sentimental items of us together. He is the gift that keeps on giving. I find new appreciation for him. I wish I had known him sooner. The Poconos are the relaxation I didn't know I needed. Since we both share a love for music, we decide to go to a record shop nearby. There is a range of vinyl records and CDs.

"Hey babe, look at all these amazing artists. I am happy we came here."

"I love it here, I don't want to leave. Listen, it's one of my fave songs, 'Put Your Records On' by Corinne Bailey Rae," I say while humming to the tune of the song.

"That's a great song, but have you heard that song 'I Want To Be Your Man' by Roger?"

Amadi begins serenading me with the song's chorus, which I think is cute.

"Okay, look who has good taste in music."

"Nah, you trying to be funny, Esi. Of course I have good taste. I'm an avid music listener."

"I guess we have that in common."

Life felt simpler back when we owned physical media. We have a very nostalgic day.

This was the first time I even went on vacation with Amadi. We wanted to take things slow and not travel together at first. This vacation goes well; we relate on a deeper level that still shocks me. I found my best friend to do life with. Don't worry, I also did something nice for his birthday in May. I take him out to eat and we also go to an indoor trampoline park because he never went before. He gets showered with tons of love that day and days leading up. I never wanted to do something heartfelt for a man before, but I guess there's a first for everything.

The months have been flying by. Before I know it, it's summer. Each month has its challenges, but brings teachable lessons. I also have the pleasure of starting my new job in the summer and while the transition has been met with some challenges, it's been smooth for the most part. Especially with the help of my coworkers. Everyone is welcoming and it is a smaller setting than I previously had. I miss my previous school for the fast-paced environment, but we all know what happens. You experience burn out quickly. I notice that the helping fields have the most burn out due to several factors, including appeasing higher-ups in the system and people expecting so much out of us while giving little resources or pay. I have compassion for what I do. God willing, I'll continue to pursue this job for the foreseeable future.

I create a personal goal of losing weight and improving my overall fitness. Amadi has kept me accountable. He is the athletic and health conscious one in the relationship. Slowly, his ways are rubbing off on me. I want to live a long life with few health problems. Something I notice is too often, black and marginalized communities have health problems that go unnoticed. Me being a black woman has impacted the way I see the healthcare system. Black women are more likely to have their symptoms overlooked. It's one of the main reasons I started to care more about my overall wellbeing. That includes my physical and mental wellness. So far, I have lost twenty pounds through prayer and discipline. I just want to lose approximately fifteen more pounds, then focus on maintenance. I'm not trying to reach a specific aesthetic. Just want to fit better in my clothes and have more endurance doing light activities. I am proud of myself for making this decision. What I notice the most is that things start working in my favor when I started having a better mindset. Having a loving partner is amazing, but the work starts from within.

Ring... Ring... Ring... My phone buzzes. I run and look at the caller ID, and it's an unfamiliar number. I let it go straight to voicemail. A few moments later, a message pops up stating that I have a new voicemail. Curiosity gets the best of me, so I listen. The biggest mistake ever. If I have an emoji to express how I feel, it would be the rolling eyes face. It was none other than Seth. Like, why? When you're doing well for yourself, people from your past come along to test you. Here's what he says.

"Hey Esi, I know I'm the last person you want to hear from. I wanted to say I'm sorry for the last interaction we had. Your assumption about me was right. I respect that you are in a relationship. Just wanted to let you know how amazing of a person you are."

This man has audacity to call me from a random number to tell me this. It's a little too late for all that. I decide to let Amadi know what's going on.

"Babe, my ex I was telling you about tried to reach out to me and left a voicemail."

"What? Really? How insane is that?"

"Somehow, he knew I was in a relationship. Talking about how he's sorry." *Sorry for yourself.*

"I know you're mad, and I am too, but he's testing the waters to see if he can come back and run the same game on you. I'm glad you didn't fall for it."

"You are right, he's trying to ruin what I have, but I'm not interested. Will be blocking his number."

"Men like him give us good guys a bad rep."

"Anyways, how's your day going?"

"It was busy. Work has its demands, but I'm relaxing now."

"Okay, look at you getting to chill. I hope you had something to eat."

"You know me now, I'm a foodie. I had some suya meat and veggies with a mixed berry smoothie."

"Oh, wow, it sounds yummy. The thought of suya makes my mouth water. I love your cooking."

"It was, but I would love to cook for you again."

"I'd love that, Amadi."

After our phone call ended, I reached out to Zuhrah via text message to give her the tea.

ESI:

Hey Girl, I have some spicy gist for you.

ZUHRAH:

Tell me what's going on. You had me at
spicy. LOL

ESI:

A random number called me, and it was none
other than Seth. I didn't pick up, so he left a
voicemail.

ZUHRAH:

The nerve of that man after he played with
your time. It's giving, 'I lost a good one now
I'm obsessed.'

ESI:

Yes. Like, I moved on, he should too.

ZUHRAH:

Men like that never forget a good woman that
got away. Anyways, forget about him. You
found an amazing man that loves you, girl.

ESI:

You're right, I'm a good woman and I am just
annoyed he still has my number. After all this
time.

ZUHRAH:

All you can do is block and go about your day.
Don't engage like he wants.

ESI:

That's exactly what I will do.

ZUHRAH:

Good, end of story. How have things been in
your relationship? Do you feel it's moving in
the right direction?

ESI:

Things have been great. The chemistry is
there, and I feel marriage is the next step.

ZUHRAH:

OMG! That is so amazing to know. He's a perfect match for you. My prayer is that it moves towards that because you deserve the world.

ESI:

Aww, thank you so much my friend.

We talked for a little while longer, but like the grandma I am, I fall asleep. I was thinking a lot yesterday. Although Seth was the last person I wanted to hear from, it put many things into perspective for me. Not only did I move on, but I did the work and healed. Something that he clearly hasn't done. The only question I have for him is, why reach out to me again if I stated not to? I am on a journey of self-love and self-worth. I have found a wonderful man that treats me with respect. Life really turned out how it was supposed to for me. The very things that brought me pain, I can now look back on and laugh because I'm no longer who I used to be. God can restore. He can renew and mend together the broken-hearted. This journey has been one wild ride and while I could've dwelled on it, I didn't for long.

I can tell I am moving towards a better future. One with love. The past few months have been a whirlwind of emotions for Anastasia. Especially having her firstborn child has been met with blessings and challenges as well. She's adjusting to motherhood and wants her privacy as she navigates through that. Having support from my mom and her mother-in-law the first few months have been beneficial to her. Watching him reach his milestones, from eating solid foods to crawling to taking his first steps, have been exciting for her. Baby Nathaniel is a joy to be around. Everyone showers that boy with love and attention. Wow, he is a momma's boy. He loves his momma for sure.

"He is a smiling baby and easy to parent. He gives me no issues apart from sleeping," as Anastasia likes to say.

The time has arrived for my family to celebrate baby Nathaniel's first birthday. So far, Anastasia has been giving up progress pictures of him monthly in the family group chat. He has grown so much. She calls him her Chunky Jo. Since he was born on a Monday, his name is

Kwadwo. Hence why that's his nickname. We have a fun time at Nathaniel's birthday. It's more for the kids, but the adults have a great time. It's safari-themed with a whole bunch of activities to keep the children entertained. According to my sister, his favorite show is *Go Deigo Go*. That's an old throwback. His outfit is so adorable. He has on a safari explorer costume with a hat. We see live animals like small mammals, reptiles and birds from the wild shown by trained professionals. Some of the kids are a bit reluctant, but for the most part, the majority would touch the various creatures present.

Nathaniel is calm and engaged for the most part, but like any child, they get a little agitated after a while. He cries once because he wants to walk on his own without being carried. He's young, so he doesn't walk well without stumbling at times. He's an independent child, Anastasia says often. She knows her kid better than anyone else. Overall, we have a blast. Thanks to my mom for organizing the party. I think about having children frequently. However, the fear remains of childbirth and raising a whole human. Saying that makes me nervous. At the same time, I am confident I wouldn't have to raise a child on my own. Amadi is a wonderful partner and would be an incredible dad. I am gushing over this man. Speaking of which, we went on an unforgettable date to the Museum of Ice Cream. I can speak for the both of us when I say it's fun. It's the little things that matter the most to me. Chill dates are the coolest. It's also the first time that Amadi and I ride the train together. What an experience being that he doesn't like it much. Having a car really is a privilege.

My family is planning a reunion with all our relatives. This is going to be remarkably interesting, being that I have not seen the majority of them since the baby shower. I would love to know where the rift in our relationship started, because before, we were all together as a unit. It's because we are all far away from each other. I feel as though God can restore this connection, and a reunion is the first step to all this. The majority of our family lives abroad anyways, so it's a little chaotic, but we will figure out something. We're also looking for a venue that can house a large family gathering. Maybe in the outskirts of New York. You know my mother is the mastermind behind everything. She's the one that came up with the idea in the first place. My only complaint is that she'll delegate tasks to me and my sisters. It's not easy being my mother's daughter. Everything must be a grand occasion.

What can I say, I can't wait to have a family of my own. We will have special gatherings and pass on our legacy. I keep having this feeling that everything will all work out. I mean, it already has. The New Year's event solidified that for me. The uncertainty I had back then is no longer there. I am proud of the steps I am taking to fulfill my purpose. I can't wait to be a mother and wife. If it's God's will for my life, it will happen, and I won't have to question a thing. We thank God for growth because the old me felt defeated, but I learned to rely on the Lord. Can't wait to see what's in store for me. Whatever it is, my life will be a glorious one and it will reflect his everlasting love for me.

EPILOGUE

A Tale that lasts forever (One year later...)

SOMETHING HAS CHANGED IN MY MAN RECENTLY. I CAN'T PUT MY finger on it, but Amadi is oddly quiet today, which is not like him. Usually, he has so much to say. This man usually tells me a lot, but it's difficult to get a read on him. He keeps checking his phone during our date. I am suspicious about it all.

"Babe, are you okay? Is everything all right?"

"Yep, I just have to make a quick call. Be right back."

While I sit at the table, thoughts are running through my mind. *Is it the day I have been anticipating? No, it can't be. Amadi would've taken me ring shopping, right? Scratch that idea, just go with the flow. I am not even wearing my best dress for the occasion. Surely this isn't happening tonight.* He comes back a few minutes later. We sit and eat in silence while he periodically checks his phone. When we're done eating, he finally speaks, clearing his throat before saying a word.

"My love, we are going to a stop on the way home."

"Okay, sounds good."

He drives to this building in a part of NYC I haven't been to and opens my door. He whispers something in my ear.

"I wanted to show you how special you are. Follow me."

We go up some stairs, and the sweet sound of music fills the air. The song becomes familiar with each step I take: it's "Best Part" by Daniel Caeser ft. H.E.R. Immediately, it all is clear to me that this is my proposal. I walk up the last step and see my family, his family, and our friends. Each of them have roses in their hands and are smiling. As if they're anticipating me coming. I become emotional. Tears begin to fill my eyes. Then there's the sign covered with a bunch of floral arrangements, which says, "It Was Always You" in neon. Once we reach the sign, Amadi gives a speech.

"Before I start, I just want to say thank you to our lovely friends and family for attending this glorious moment."

He turns to look at me and says, "Esi, I have known you for some time. Every moment with you has been uplifting. You give me reasons to love you more. There was never a time I was uncertain about you. I knew we'd get to this point in our journey. You make me better. I will keep loving you till the end."

I couldn't stop the tears from flowing. *This can't be real.* I remain stunned, unable to speak. In my mind, the song "See What the Lord Has Done" by Nathaniel Bassey keeps repeating. *This the moment I have been waiting for.* God has been so faithful to me and brought a man I didn't have to ask to love me properly. He sent a man after his own heart. Amadi pulls out a jewelry box from his pocket and gets on one knee.

"It has always been you, Esi. My Omalicha. Will you marry me?"

I smile and say, "Yes."

He places the ring on my finger. There's clapping and cheering from the crowd. I could hear my mother.

"Show us the ring!" she says.

I move my hands towards everyone and begin wiggle my hands as the ring glistens in the light. All the while, I'm just realizing the photographer and videographer capturing this moment.

Amadi has surpassed my wildest dreams. I always wanted an intimate proposal with people near and dear to my heart. I turn to Amadi and ask, "How long have you been planning this proposal?"

"I started this five months ago, but I bought the ring months prior."

"Wow, you kept a secret this long. Who helped?"

"Zuhrah, of course."

I look around, trying to spot my bestie. "So, you knew and didn't say anything?" I say with a laugh.

She nods in agreeance with the question. "Sis Ayeeko."

The outpouring of love still has me in shock. I embrace everyone and thank them for coming. I even see Nadira there as well, which was a shock to me, being that I mentioned her once.

"Hey girlie, I am so happy for you. Your moment has come, and God has shined his light upon you."

We hugged and it felt great being surrounded by my people.

"Thank you, Nadira. Isn't God good."

Amadi gives me a beautiful bouquet of roses that says in bold cursive, "She Said Yes." I look at him again and say, "Babe, I love you. Thank you for making this moment extraordinary for me."

My sisters come to me and fix my makeup so I can take some suitable pictures. I take pictures with everyone, taking in the moment.

"She's a wifey. Show us your ring," Gabrielle says.

My two other sisters, Ivy and Anastasia, give me praises.

"Ahoɔfɛ Esi," my sisters are chanting.

The ring is a rectangle diamond cut with vines with smaller stones wrapping around it.

"It's the most unique ring I've ever seen. Wow, my future son-in-law has expensive taste," my mom utters. We all laugh as she says that.

"Thank you, ma," he says.

"My daughter is finally getting her happy ending." My dad walks up to me and gives me the biggest hug.

My dad is a man of little words, but when he speaks, you listen, because you know he means every word.

Momma and Papa Damilare come up to me and say, "Why don't we get a picture of you two cutting the cake?"

Amadi holds my hand to guide me to the table with a heart-shaped cake. We cut the cake and feed it to one another. This is a surreal moment. *What one man was hesitant to do, a man always knew he would.* I feel fulfilled. Grateful sums up all my emotions. I look at my ring, smiling because it was worth the hurdles I had to overcome. The rest of the night consists of spending quality time together as a couple.

Two weeks later, and I am still in awe of what happened. Butterflies in my tummy tell of my current state. I'm a fiancée, wow. Amadi and I have been deciding the venue. Dealing with wedding planning will be a headache, so I've consulted a professional to assist me. My mom has been the best at giving advice, but she is burnt out from the family reunion we had. There were a hundred family members in attendance. My dad's side of the family is very chill, while my mom's family is boisterous and outgoing. My dad wasn't really a fan of the reunion. To him, it was a waste of money, but he neglected to admit he enjoyed himself regardless. He got to reconnect with his family. It meant the world to me, seeing him laugh. Can I say it was an interesting time. I got to reconnect with my cousins, uncles, and aunts, but it was hectic. There were activities to keep us all entertained. The last full night was a sneaker ball to celebrate coming together as a unit. I danced the most. I was the life of the party.

I told Amadi this and he stated, "I hope you have this type of energy when we get married."

Challenge accepted. If he thought Zuhrah's wedding was my best moves, wait until he sees the routine I have for us.

Finally, I can say the news that I have been keeping secret for the past few weeks. Zuhrah is pregnant! She found out at around 6 weeks. My friend swore me to secrecy. It was difficult because I wanted to disclose the news to my mom and sisters. Knowing my mom, the whole town would've known. The Ghanaian community is quite big in some parts of NYC, so word would've traveled fast. I respect my friend's privacy. She announces it on social media on a beach in Puerto Rico with the caption Baby Bamidele Loading embroidered on a baby onesie. They both are holding each end. It wouldn't be her if she didn't announce it on her own terms. She's the most extra person I know, next to my mother and fiancé. Especially being that it's her first child. Some people dream of having the gift of pregnancy even once in their lives. I'm going to be a godmother for the first time.

Amadi and I are in the process of buying a home together. Ideally, I will move to New Jersey. I am ready for a new journey that awaits us. This is a big step for us, being that we'll be homeowners for the first time. We're still deciding on the location. However, we've toured some modern and cozy places. One day, we will buy land to build our own home. We're not sure what state we'll live in the future, but I am working on being licensed as a speech pathologist over there. Again, I am changing jobs, but I feel as though it's for the best. Maybe God wants me to work through my discomfort of switching jobs. Being in a new environment is scary because of the uncertainty of how things will go. I can't believe I am saying this out loud. This year, I wanted to learn how to drive. It's perfect timing. I have entered my thirties feeling like an empowered agent of change. Amadi is helping me achieve that goal. He's been teaching me the basics in areas with less traffic. I am truly blessed to have him as my personal cheerleader. He's patient, kind, and loving. Can't wait to spend forever with him.

* * *

Thank you for taking the time out to read my book. I hope you enjoyed it. If you are interested in signing up for my newsletter, I have put the link down below.

https://mailchi.mp/f73d61f4c2cd/aqueensdiaries-email-sign-up

BOOKS BY THE AUTHOR

Becoming Afua Osei

About the Author

The author Mary Mensah received her bachelor's degree from SUNY Plattsburgh in Upstate NY. She majored in psychology with a double minor in gender & women's studies and communication sciences and disorders. She then went to SUNY Oswego where she got her masters in school counseling. Mental health counseling is her current passion which she hopes to pursue further. In her free time, she loves to watch YouTube and tv shows such as A Different World. She enjoys furthering her knowledge and has a passion for mental health.

instagram.com/aqueensdiaries_96

facebook.com/mary.mensah.35

tiktok.com/@aqueensdiaries_96

youtube.com/@Ohemaamary

goodreads.com/marymensah_96

amazon.com/author/marymensah_96

threads.com/@aqueensdiaries_96

9 798990 406254